Alpha's Command

Shifter Ops

Renee Rose

Lee Savino

Copyright © November 2022 Alpha's Command by Renee Rose and Lee Savino

All rights reserved. This copy is intended for the original purchaser of this e-book ONLY. No part of this e-book may be reproduced, scanned, or distributed in any printed or electronic form without prior written permission from the author. Please do not participate in or encourage piracy of copyrighted materials in violation of the author's rights. Purchase only authorized editions.

Published in the United States of America

Midnight Romance, LLC

This e-book is a work of fiction. While reference might be made to actual historical events or existing locations, the names, characters, places and incidents are either the product of the author's imaginations or are used fictitiously, and any resemblance to actual persons, living or dead, business establishments, events, or locales is entirely coincidental.

This book contains descriptions of many BDSM and sexual practices, but this is a work of fiction and, as such, should not be used in any way as a guide. The author and publisher will not be responsible for any loss, harm, injury, or death resulting from use of the information contained within. In other words, don't try this at home, folks!

Want FREE books?

Go to http://subscribepage.com/alphastemp to sign up for Renee Rose's newsletter and receive a free books. In addition to the free stories, you will also get special pricing, exclusive previews and news of new releases.

Download a free Lee Savino book from www.leesavino.com

Chapter One

hanning
    I prowl on four paws through the pine trees, closing in on the house. It's a small split-level, set back from the road and surrounded by trees. The lot's on the end of a cul-de-sac, and the backyard abuts the Coconino National Forest. Plenty of wilderness, plenty of cover to run. My wolf approves.

So did my brother when he bought it fourteen years ago and settled with his newly pregnant mate. When life was good and the future was bright.

Then he died, and everything changed.

Almost everything. The house still looks the same. She's taken good care of it. The paint has faded, and the roof will need replacing, but otherwise, it's frozen in time.

The scents are the same—juniper and boxelder, pine.

The wind picks up, and I catch another scent, one I'm trying not to notice. It curls into my senses, a delicious perfume that makes my fangs sharpen, and my mouth waters.

Lilac and lavender.

My Kryptonite.

My wolf wants to cross the fifty feet separating us from the house, to find the source of the perfume and bask in it.

Instead, I turn and trot on silent paws past the house, up the hill where a Ponderosa pine stretches to the sky. I still remember the day we climbed the hill. I admired the view of Mount Elden, but my brother only had eyes for his house. For his human wife and young son playing on the patio.

Promise me, my brother demanded all those years ago. He had an army training position at Camp Navajo, but he'd been sought out for active duty by someone who knew what he was. Someone who needed his kind in the field. Just for a short-term mission.

I rub against the pine bark, searching for any lingering scent of him.

And then I catch it–a rich male wolf musk. It smells like my brother, but he's dead. Which means it must belong to Geo, his son.

My nephew's been running through these woods.

That means he's shifted. We weren't sure whether he would. Mixing shifter blood with a human's can wipe out the shifting ability in offspring, but puberty hormones must've kicked Geo's wolf-shifter genes to life.

Which means I can no longer stay away. Julia won't know how to guide her son through this.

Geo needs me.

Looking closer, I catch sight of claw marks on the tree,

like Geo was tormented by his new shape. Frustrated and alone.

Fuck.

Deke expects me at the job site, and if I'm late, he'll be pissed. More pissed than usual. I'll have to come back in the morning, as soon as this mission is complete.

I lope down the hill and head the long way around the house. A light turns on in the upstairs bedroom, and for a moment, a woman's silhouette appears. Everything in me longs to change plans and head back to the house. Make sure the door is locked. Make sure she's safe.

Instead, I turn and run away from temptation.

Away from the only woman I've ever wanted.

The only woman I can't have.

* * *

I zoom up to the row of abandoned warehouses at midnight. Right on time.

Deke waits in an old van painted matte black. The sort of van that workmen use... or kidnappers. We got the van after a mission that involved a hostage situation if I remember correctly.

I park my bike and rap on the van's side door. "Hey, man, got any free candy?"

Deke rolls down the window but doesn't answer—just frowns at me. He's got "resting murder face" as Lana, Teddy's new mate, likes to call it.

"You look like a serial killer," I tell him. He glowers harder. "What? It's a compliment."

"Why were you late?" he growls. "You left Taos before I did."

"Pit stop." I waggle my brows, so he'll look away, disgusted. Let him think I was at a bar, hitting on the ladies, making any lingering lavender and lilac scent unimportant. No way I'm telling him where I really was.

"This the place?" I nod to the farthest warehouse, built right up against the forest. This whole commercial strip is quiet at night, but there's a light on above that warehouse door. Every once in a while, a shadowy figure glides from the forest and slips inside.

Deke drums his fingers on the steering wheel. "GPS says so."

"Let me go in first, do some reconnaissance. I got a hookup." I hold up my phone, where I've been texting with the fight club organizers.

"What if the targets make you?"

"They're not targets. They're kids."

"Teenagers," Deke grumbles, his eyes penetrating the darkness. "Why am I on babysitting duty?"

"Hey, this is good practice. You know your mate Sadie is going to want a full house."

The name of his mate softens his expression, as I knew it would.

"Picture it," I say as I reach up, hands framing the pretend screen, to distract myself from the bite of longing in my own chest and to keep him from picking up on my feelings. "You, Sadie, seven pups—"

"Seven?" His black brows fly up as if picturing this scene I'm painting.

"Yeah, and they're rolling around on the floor, biting your boots." I grin at the alarm spreading from Deke's eyes through his facial expression. "Has Sadie not told you how many kids she wants?"

"Two to four," he says slowly.

"There you go," I grin. "You have four kids. Throw in a set of twins or triplets, a few surprises. Happy accidents. It'll be great."

Deke's Adam's apple bobs, and his hands squeeze the steering wheel. He looks ready to throw the van in reverse and race out of here.

"Daddy Deke." I smile to fan the fire, and he looks at me like he wants to run me over as he flees the scene.

My work done, I slap the side of the van like a big exclamation point and saunter towards the warehouse as if I've got nothing on my mind but this little rescue mission.

More people stream into the side door. A quiet commercial strip with an abandoned building right near the forest is the perfect place to host a pop-up shifter fight club. The organizers, Trey and Jared, have a regular place in Tucson, Arizona. But tonight's fight is special.

A pack of acid-green Kawasaki ninjas zooms past me. They go from sixty to zero, sending up a spray of gravel as they park. The gangly bikers dismount and huddle together. Werecheetahs. I can spot them a mile away. They like fast bikes and tight leather.

A few glance at me as I pass, their eyes flashing green. I pretend to ignore them, avoiding eye contact. My wolf is riled up after stopping by Julia's. He wants to go back and claim what he thinks is his. I won't let him, so he's itching for a fight.

More shifters have flocked to the warehouse and are hanging around the door. I walk through a cloud of smoke and musky scents.

A familiar wolf shifter steps outside and surveys the crowd. He's wearing jeans, scuffed motorcycle boots, and a white t-shirt under a leather jacket. The only difference between his outfit and mine is the insignia on the jacket–a snarling wolf with the words 'Tucson Pack' emblazoned underneath. "Fight starting in twenty," he announces and stands aside to let his customers hurry inside.

I step out of the shadows, and he clocks my scent. We both grin and step forward to slap each other on the back.

"Jared," I greet him.

"Channing, my brother. Glad you could make it."

"I'm here on business," I remind him. "Package pick up."

"Right. They're inside. Trey's been keeping an eye on them. You sure they can't stay? They're adults."

"They're barely eighteen. You know how young shifters are."

"Yeah." Jared blows out a breath. "But part of me thinks they just need role models."

"They have five older brothers. Their brothers would be here themselves, but Matthias is busy at the hospital, and Teddy and Darius are away on business. Separate business," I add before Jared asks if Teddy made up with his twin brother. "Darius is in New York. Teddy's in L.A. with his new mate."

"I heard he got a mate. Your whole pack's found their mates, what... just this year?"

"Last twelve months," I say. "Yup. The whole pack."

Except me.

"Nice," Jared says.

"How's Angelina?" I ask before he can ask about my mate situation.

His face softens like Deke's did when I mention his mate. "She's great. Real great. Back in Tucson getting ready for a show. Her troupe's performing this weekend."

"I can't believe you came all the way up here for a fight club. You've got a sweet place in Tucson."

"Full house every night," he says with satisfaction. "But Sheridan's making it more of a hipster beer bar thing. Sometimes we miss the old vibe, so we do these pop-up clubs. We found this abandoned strip. Thought it'd be perfect." He directs me inside, and the thick miasma of scents hits me. Weed, beer, unwashed shifters of all sorts. The big, open space is crowded with people, hazy with smoke and sawdust. The only lights are two spotlights trained on the ring in the center of the room. The crowd mills about, murmuring, betting, craning their necks to spot the fighters. The place hums with anticipation.

A trio of shifters stand in one corner, taking bets. Their scents are weird, a mishmash of animals. The tallest of them, a painfully thin white guy with bottle cap glasses, sneezes and delicate white feathers puff out of his jacket. He catches me staring at him and sneezes again. More feathers fly. His buddies pat his back without looking up from their notebooks.

I jerk my chin up in a reverse nod to signal that everything's cool.

"They're over there." Jared points to a shadowy corner beyond the fighting ring. "With Caleb. He's the headline fight tonight."

"I thought Caleb retired? Lives up in the mountains with his mate?"

"He does. We talked him into one fight. That's why we did the pop-up here near Flagstaff–he was already in the area. His mate is doing some research on Grand Canyon trees. Some science shit. Otherwise, he wouldn't come. No fun being on the road when you have a beautiful mate waiting for you at home."

"I bet," I say.

He glances at me, and I keep my expression light and casual. Is he remembering that I'm the only one in the pack without a mate? Is there pity in his eyes?

"I better pick up the packages before they get into trouble. Thanks, man." We share another back slap, and I head toward the corner. All this talk about mates has my wolf on edge. That's part of the reason I volunteered for this mission. Everyone in my pack is mated up. Even Lance, former fuck boy, is happily settled down with a mate and a baby girl.

I weave through the clusters of shifters to the back where the fighters are waiting to be called. The packages–the three teens I'm supposed to pick up and carry home safely–stand in a knot around one of the most famous fighters.

A sharp scent of clove tickles my nose. Someone's wearing clove cologne. A shifter only does that when trying to hide their scent.

The clove perfume clears as I reach the trio of teens, and I get a face full of werebear teenager funk. The three skinny young men are identical triplets in an awkward teenage growth phase. Their arms and legs are stick thin, but their feet and hands are huge. They're going to be taller than their brothers Axel, Teddy and Darius. Maybe even Matthias. But not Everest. And it'll take a lot of food to bulk them up to fighting weight.

Not that I'm going to fight them.

The three triplets throng around a huge dude with a scary-ass beard. Another werebear named Caleb. The headline fighter.

"It was so awesome," one of the triplets tells Caleb. This one is wearing a red kilt but no shirt. "You went two rounds and then *bam*." The teen mimics an uppercut punch, complete with sound effects. "*Whap*, left hook, right hook,"

"It was a haymaker," another triplet puts in. Bern, I think his name is. Bern is dressed in all-black head-to-toe, including Doc Martens and a black-on-black plaid kilt.

"Right, a haymaker," the shirtless triplet says. I'm pretty sure his name is Canyon. "And then you slammed into the ropes and then–"

"Another haymaker," puts in the third triplet. He's in a red plaid kilt and a white tunic-like shirt with billowing sleeves–like a pirate's. Hutch, his family calls him.

"Yeah," says Canyon. His Adam's apple wobbles as he shadow-boxes. "And then he falls, and it was epic–"

"Yeah, I know," Caleb says. "I was there." His huge beard hides his expression, but I sense his amusement.

"We didn't see the fight, but our brother did and told us.

We came all the way from Bad Bear Mountain," says Canyon. "We're your biggest fans."

"Hey, guys." I lean in and slap Bern and Hutch on the back, getting a grip of their t-shirts. "Your brother, Matthias, wants to know why you didn't show up to class today."

The triplets stiffen. Canyon glances across the warehouse to the single entrance or exit but doesn't run. If he does, I'll cuff his two brothers and then text Deke.

"You're not supposed to be here," I say. "Shifter Fight Club is twenty-one and older."

"No one's checking IDs," Hutch protests.

"We're almost nineteen," Bern adds. "That's at least twenty-one in shifter years."

"You're nineteen?" I ask. They act younger, but Teddy told me their puberty was rough with their animals taking over and forcing them to shift. Their ma had to homeschool them. They've been sheltered from the outside world. No wonder they sound so naive.

"We're late bloomers," Hutch says, his voice cracking. "Darius told us he and Teddy were exactly the same. Late puberty."

The triplets nod in unison.

Caleb watches our interchange closely. "How do they know their brother sent you?"

"Brothers, plural. Check your phones," I order the triplets.

"I forgot mine." Canyon crosses his arms across his shirtless chest. He's going to be a handful.

Bern and Hutch have already fished their phones out of the small pouches they're wearing at their waist. There are

Alpha's Command

tons of texts from their brothers Matthias, Teddy, and Darius, including a picture of me. "This is Channing. Go with him and do what he says," I recite one of the texts.

Hutch shows it to Caleb, who nods.

"You heard him, boys." Caleb says. "You can see me fight when you're a little older."

The triplets deflate.

"But you're retired," Hutch says mournfully.

"Officially. I'll talk to Jared and Trey and schedule something for two years from now."

"You would do that?" Canyon asks. "For us?"

"Yep. You're my biggest fans." Caleb jerks his chin in my direction. With one last slap on Canyon's shoulder, he heads off into the gloom.

In the center of the ring, Jared calls for the first two fighters to take their places. Spectators press close to the ring.

"Come on, we gotta go," I say.

"Can we just see one fight?" Hutch pleads. "Please?"

I hesitate. What will one little fight hurt? But something tugs in me, so I don't pause. "Your brothers want you back. They said you've been acting suspicious for weeks. Drinking giant protein shakes and streaming Rocky movies nonstop."

"That's not suspicious."

"Yeah, we always do that."

In the ring, two fighters circle each other. One's a cheetah shifter, I can tell by the way his pack—or *coalition* in cheetah-speak--presses close to the ropes and shouts encouragement. Jared and another lanky wolf shifter, a tall guy with a mohawk and big ear gauges, keep telling the cheetahs to move back.

"First fight is Speed Ballz versus Benny the Biter," Hutch says, pointing to a big chalkboard over by the bookies. Speed Ballz is such a cheetah biker name.

My eye catches on the names scrawled in a fight lower down. "The Kilted Killers?" I read, and the triplets freeze. "Does that mean what I think it does?"

Hutch and Bern hang their heads.

"We wanted to fight," Canyon says. "Some guy challenged us."

"He said if we lost, we'd owe him a favor," Hutch pipes up.

"What the fuck? That's not how shifter fights work. What guy?"

The triplets shrug in perfect unison. Their movements are so similar, it's like they choreographed them.

"Enough of this." I point to the warehouse door. I'll have to herd them through the crowd. "Start walking."

Canyon mutters something I don't catch, but the three obediently turn and tromp towards the door. I direct them along a path on the periphery of the warehouse. The fight is in full force, and the warehouse shakes with shouts. Then Benny the Biter gives into his nickname and tries to eat his opponent and is disqualified. The crowd deflates, except for the cheetahs, who carry their hero on their shoulders out the door.

"Hang on," I order the triplets. We're almost to the door, but the cheetahs are swamping it. "Let's wait a second."

Got the package, I text Deke. *We'll be out in five.*

10-4. He texts back. *Any hostiles?*

No.

Alpha's Command

Jared steps into the ring, announcing the next match. The cheetahs are almost all out of the door. The triplets wait beside me, their eyes glued longingly to the chalkboard. Calebs' fight is last. Too bad. It's tempting to allow the Terrible Threes to stay and watch him. Jared's right, teens need role models.

We're close enough I can read the name on the giant chalkboard opposite the "Kilted Killers." Some guy named Hannibal. Not a fighter I've heard of before.

I signal to the gray-headed bookie and point to the Kilted Killers' fight. "Can you remove that match? These guys are forfeiting."

The bookie nods and signals his tall, feathery friend to cross out the fight.

"Next time, guys," I tell the triplets, who look mournful. "By the way, what's with the kilts?" I ask Hutch.

"Our mother is a MacDonald," Hutch informs me glumly.

The way to the door is clear, so I signal them to keep moving. We step out into the night air. More cars have filled the parking lot. Beyond them, the cheetahs have built a big bonfire in the center of their assembled bikes.

"Hey," Canyon asks. "Are you on your bike?"

"Yeah," I say.

"How are we getting home if you're on your bike?" Bern asks.

"How did you get here?" I return.

"We hitchhiked," Hutch pipes up. His two brothers shoot him a dirty look.

"You hitchhiked." I shake my head. I'll have to tell Teddy. He'll shit a brick.

"We can steal some bikes and ride with you." Canyon's looking longingly at the cheetah's crotch rockets. "We know how to hotwire–"

"No stealing. No bikes. We're not riding. Come on, Deke is waiting in the van."

The Terrible Threes stop as one. "The creeper van?" one asks.

"Uh, yeah." I hide a smile.

"Awesome," says Bern. Hutch and Canyon exchange high fives.

"Wait," I say. "Are you excited to ride in the back of the creeper van?"

"Yeah!"

"Duh."

"Stoked!"

I shake my head. Teenagers. No use trying to understand them. "Let's go," I order. Deke is parked in the same place. I could text him, but he can't pull the van up much closer than he is now. To the right are a bunch of parked cars and more shifters on Harleys beyond that. To the left is the forest. "We have to pass the cheetah pack."

"Coalition," Hutch says. "A group of cheetahs is called a coalition."

"Right. We'll have to pass the coalition. Keep your eyes averted. Hide your fangs. No posing, no challenging."

We're almost to the bonfire when a giant steps out from a set of parked cars and blocks our path. Beefy dude with black shades. The giant stands between us and the cheetah bonfire.

Alpha's Command

I can't tell because of the flickering firelight, but the skin outside of his sunglasses looks scarred up. Weird. It takes a lot of effort to get a shifter to scar like that. The only way I know to scar a shifter is to use vampire blood.

Who is this guy? I take a big sniff and end up getting a noseful of clove cologne. The scent numbs my nose to the point my sense of smell is useless. *Asshole.*

Behind me, the triplets have gone still.

"Hey man," I say. "Not to be rude, but you're wearing sunglasses at night."

The triplets titter behind me, but the clove-scented poser in front of me gives no answer.

"No? Okay, I respect your fashion choices."

"They promised me a fight," the man rumbles, pointing a finger at the werebears behind me.

"Hannibal?" I ask, guessing his name from the fighter listed as the Kilted Killers opponent. The giant nods. "They're too young. And they're not in your weight class."

"I know," Hannibal tilts his head and cracks his thick neck. "Was gonna fight three on one."

I shrug. "Too bad. Wait a few years and these kids–" I toss a thumb over my shoulder, "–can do whatever they want. But tonight, it's not happening."

The party at the bonfire is heating up. More cat shifters have shown up on their crotch rockets. A few pass us, smelling of weed and grain alcohol. Two wereleopards–I can tell they're leopards because who the fuck else would wear a leopard print leather jacket?–head over with jugs of gasoline. The cats pour the liquid on the flames, and yellow-blue plumes shoot up to the sky. Whoops and hollers echo around the parking lot. Sounds like there's a werehyena or two in the mix.

I need to get these three kids across the parking lot, past the bonfire and the drunken revelers, safely into the van with Deke. But Hannibal isn't having it. He stands, legs apart, feet planted, seven feet and three hundred and fifty pounds of pure muscle.

"Okay, man," I roll my shoulders. "You want to fight? You got one."

"You?" Hannibal barks.

"I know, I'm out of your weight class, but we'll make it work."

"Too easy," he sneers. "I fight you and the three."

"These three have somewhere to be," I say. I'm backing up a little, putting space between me and the obstacle, hoping the triplets will get the hint. They do. The three move with me. "But I have a friend who will join us. What do you say? Two on one?"

"What friend?"

I point to my pocket. "Can I call him?" I don't wait for permission. I fish the phone out of my pocket and hit Deke's number. He answers with a grunt.

"Hostiles." I stare Hannibal down as I speak. "Initiate the Berlin maneuver."

"Ten-four." Deke ends the call.

"What–" Hannibal starts, and I whip out my Glock and shoot out his knees.

"Run," I shout, over Hannibal's bellows. I chop a hand through the air to show the direction they should go. "To the van."

The triplets take off. Bern in the lead, Hutch and Canyon at his heels.

Hannibal is on the pavement, propped on his arms. His sunglasses have fallen off, and when he looks up, his eye area is a mass of scars. Instead of shifter bright, his eyes are black.

I whirl and race to catch up with the triplets.

A bullet won't stop a shifter for long. We just slowed him down.

Worse, the shot drew the attention of the cats. I careen into one, and the cat shifter hisses.

"'Scuse me," I mutter, but there's a gun in my hand.

"No dogs allowed," the cat shouts. "Stop him!"

A dozen heads turn, their green eyes like lasers seeking me out. Ahead of me, the triplets thread through bikers. They're almost to the bonfire, and the crowd is thick.

Canyon slows and looks back.

"No," I order him. "Keep going." I point my Glock in the air and fire a warning shot. The cats around me snarl and hunch like they're about to pounce.

Deke revs the van, and it leaps over a low concrete barrier and heads for the bonfire. Cats scatter. At the last second, Deke hauls the van right and crashes into the line of bikes.

The cats yowl.

"Go, go, go," I scream to Canyon. His brothers reach the back of the van and dive between the open doors.

Deke shouts something. There are too many bikes and cars in the way for him to get the van closer to us. We have to cross the parking lot to him.

There's a cheetah in my face. I duck and rush him,

plowing like a linebacker into my opponent's middle. Claws rip at my leather jacket. I drop and toss the shifter into a group of his buddies. More snarls.

The cat shifters are closing in.

"Channing," Canyon shouts. He throws something. Glass shatters and the scent of fire and grain alcohol flares around me. Flames cut into the night.

The cat next to me screeches, making my ears ring. It races past its brethren, its jacket alight.

Where did Canyon get the ingredients to make Molotov cocktails? I punch the closest cheetah and flip him over my shoulder, sending him crashing into his coalition.

Deke's doing evasive maneuvers in the van. The vehicle has a lot more horsepower than you'd expect, but the cheetahs are swarming it.

"Go," I holler, waving my arms.

Hutch sticks his head out of the window. "Canyon!"

Canyon's got his back up against the fire, a second jug of grain alcohol in his hand. He's caught in a circle of hissing cats.

Shit. This kid. I knew he would be trouble.

Light and shadow lick Canyon's bare torso. A nearby cat lunges, and he steps back, his boot crunching on glass. His kilt is dangerously close to the flames. One more step back, and he'll be in the fire.

Two were-leopards leap close. I raise my gun to warn them off.

"Coward," one hisses. "You don't bring a gun to a claw fight."

You do if you're street smart. That's where Hannibal

made a mistake. He thought I'd act like we were in a fight club match. Outside of the ring, rules don't apply.

They don't apply in the ring, either, if you don't care about losing. Or getting disqualified.

A group of shifters join the leopards. "You can't shoot us all," one says, and his buddies all cackle, raising a bottle of grain alcohol in mock toast. Werehyenas. "How many bullets do you have left?"

"Enough." I shoot the bottle, then whirl and sprint away, chased by yowling leopards. I reach the line of fallen bikes and haul one up. Normally, I'd need time to hotwire it, but this is a cheetah bike. It's already been hotwired. I tweak the proper wires, and it roars to life.

The wereleopards leap, too late. I hurtle away, heading towards the bonfire. Cats scream and fly out of my way. I throttle the thing until the front tire leaves the ground and zoom closer. Canyon's on the opposite side, the firelight painting his bare back. I'll have to fight through the flocks of shifters to get around the bonfire to him.

Or...

There's a piece of plywood propped at an angle on this side of the fire. A ramp. That was the werecheetah's plan for tonight. The dummies were going to jump the fire.

I rev the bike to breakneck speeds and zip up the ramp. The bike and I soar through the air. Heat hits my face–I'm over the fire.

I'm heavier than a werecheetah, and I didn't get a proper head start. I might not make it. The flames reach up to grab my boots.

"Canyon," I roar. And I rise, leaping off the bike–shifting into a wolf mid-air.

My body contorts, tightens, and rips out of my jeans and leather jacket. Shreds of my clothes rain onto the bonfire.

The bike crashes down, half in, half out of the fire. Right on top of where Canyon was standing–if he hadn't moved.

I land on my paws and shoot forward, ducking my wolf head, so I slide between Canyon's legs and bounce him onto my back. He shouts and falls forward, gripping my white fur. I let him ride me like a toddler riding a miniature pony all the way to the back of the parking lot, heading for my bike.

Behind us, there's a blast as flames find the crashed bike's fuel tank and explodes.

Two leopards and hyenas, their faces raw but already healing, leap out in front of me. Canyon throws the remaining Molotov cocktail at their feet, and I dash by.

Once I'm beside my bike, Canyon jumps off, and I shift back to human form. The military makes us wear these tight-fitting suit things that conform to our shift, and for once I'm grateful. It would suck to ride a bike buck-naked.

Hashtag shifter problems.

I will have to ride barefoot. My boots are toast. I shake out my hands. When I leaped from the bike, I landed in glass and some shards got caught in my paws. Shifting back to human form helped to push the glass pieces out of my skin. My feet and palms tingle, signaling that my shifter healing has kicked in.

I throw a leg over my bike and key in a complicated code to start it. No one can hotwire my bike; I have too many fail safes.

"Hop on," I order. As soon as Canyon scrambles onto the back of the bike, I throttle it forward, away from the commotion.

A few cheetahs dive in our direction, but I weave around them. Deke makes fun of my crotch rocket, but for speed and maneuverability, nothing compares. I end up swerving past the warehouse, right as the three bookie shifters come out. The bird shifter blinks behind his huge glasses and twitches, producing a cloud of white feathers. His buddy clutches his gray hair.

The third one looks delighted. "Jay-sus," he says in a thick Irish accent. "It's anarchy."

And it is. The parking lot is a mass of howling cat shifters and scorched pavement, ridden with flames.

I'll have to text an apology to Jared and Trey.

"Hang on," I bark to Canyon and rev the bike to leap a low concrete barrier and then another. We dodge a cluster of werepanthers sitting on the hoods of their pimped-out Honda Civics. They hiss but don't make a move to follow us.

There's only one road in and out of this commercial block. We catch up to Deke and the others as the van turns onto the main road.

"Whoohoo, home free," Canyon whoops.

A roar blasts at our back. Canyon hunches against me.

"Oh no," he says, his voice cracking midway through.

I risk a glance back.

Hannibal's behind us on a bike of his own. His sunglasses are back on his face. His jeans are torn and stained at the knee, but there's no other evidence that I shot him.

The bullets might as well have been dual mosquito bites for all it stopped him.

He roars again, coming for us. He's on a huge hog that looks modified somehow. For all its bulk, the bike's wicked fast.

"Hold tight," I say to Canyon, and he does. He's ridden on the back of a bike before, thank fates. I zoom up to Deke in the van. "Hostile," I shout. "Hostile six o'clock."

"Ten-four," Deke growls. He leadfoots the van onto the main road, but he won't be fast enough to outrun Hannibal. I zoom back behind the van, guarding the rear.

"What do we do?" Canyon shouts.

We? "You were supposed to go with your brothers," I snarl.

"You needed help." Canyon's arms tighten around me as we lean into a curve. "Never leave a man behind."

"You're not in the military." I glance behind us again. Hannibal is gaining.

"That's only because they won't let me join," Canyon bawls into my ear.

Fair enough. "Where did you get the Molotov cocktails?"

"Some guy was making them. I took them off his hands." Canyon twists and reports. "He's catching up."

We're on a long stretch of road. No civilians. I could stop the bike and stand my ground, give Deke a chance to escape, but that'll put Canyon in danger. I lost my gun when I shifted.

I'm out of ideas.

"What is that shifter?" Canyon asks.

"I don't know. He hid his scent with clove oil."

"So that's why I couldn't smell him. My nose went numb."

"Yeah." My voice is growing hoarse with all the ridiculous shouting, but I want to continue the conversation. I want Canyon to understand. Not sure why I want to teach the kid, but I do. "He's hiding something," I explain, leaning into another turn. Deke has to slow the van to make it, and we lose another few yards to Hannibal. "He doesn't want us to know what he is."

"Fuck," Canyon mutters softly.

Hannibal's almost on us.

The van doors fly open. Hutch and Bern are there, bracing on either side of a rocket launcher.

I nod to them, but keep my bike between them and Hannibal, right in the enemy's line of sight.

We go around another curve. Deke whips through it. Hannibal's a few feet away, his noisy hog ripping the air. Once we're on a straight stretch of road, Deke slows.

"Clear!" Bern shouts, and I zip Canyon and I out of their way. The rocket sizzles past us. There's a boom and the heat of an explosion hits the back of my neck.

Canyon laughs.

I pull alongside the van, holding steady.

"Did they get him?" I ask.

"They got his bike," Canyon says.

"Even better." I grin and give Deke a thumbs-up. He nods, and we slow to cruising speed. Hannibal's roar echoes at our backs as we speed away into the night.

Chapter Two

Channing

"I can't believe you let them shoot a rocket launcher," I say to Deke. The van's pulled over on the side of the road, and Canyon has rejoined his brothers.

Deke grunts.

I'm wearing the high-tech boxer shorts developed by the military to cling in place, even after we shift. I pull on an extra pair of sweatpants I keep in my bike's cargo hold along with my wallet. The space is too small to fit much else, so I still need a shirt, jacket, and boots.

Hashtag shifter problems.

"I guess it turned out okay." I stuff the thin military suit into the cargo hold and shut it. "You going to be okay to get these guys home?"

Deke glowers at the triplets, who are retelling their parts in tonight's mission to each other, adding more blood and guns. "Where are you going?"

"Private mission. I already cleared it with Rafe." I keep

my tone light, but my chest tightens, and I catch the ghostly whiff of a lilac and lavender scent.

Deke frowns but says nothing.

"Hey, Deke." Canyon gallops to his side. "Can I shoot the rocket launcher next?"

Deke glares at me as if to say *I can't believe you're sticking me with werebear-sitting duty.* "No."

"But what if that guy Hannibal comes back?" Hutch asks.

"You run," I say. "You're probably faster than him on foot."

Canyon opens his mouth, and I snap, "That's an order."

"Sir, yessir!" Canyon and his brothers stiffen and toss sloppy salutes.

"See," I say to Deke. "You'll be fine." I mount my bike. My feet are gonna freeze in the wind, but what am I going to do?

"Where are your boots?" Canyon asks, zeroing in on my bare feet.

"Lost 'em when I shifted over the fire," I answer, leaving out the rest of the explanation. *Because I had to save your ass. Again.*

Canyon's ears turn pink. "Here." He kicks off his boots. "It's the least I can do."

I dismount and shove my feet into them. Turns out they're close to my size, a bit bigger. "Thanks."

Canyon grins.

Hutch sticks his head out of the van's passenger side window. "Want my shirt?"

I narrow my eyes at the poofy pirate shirt. "No thanks."

Alpha's Command

Bern offers his, but it's similar to Hutch's except in black. I pass.

Deke heads to the van and pulls out a bomber jacket, brown leather with a shearling wool lining. He tosses it at me.

"What's this?" I ask.

"An extra. Take it," Deke says. "You can't ride shirtless."

I could but it'd be weird. "Appreciate it, brother." I put on the jacket, flip up the collar and hold out my arms. "How do I look?"

The triplets snicker. I'm in borrowed boots, jacket, sweatpants, and nothing else. There are better outfits to wear to a reunion that's ten years overdue, but beggars can't be choosers. No clothes shop is going to be open before dawn, and my instincts tell me to get back to Julia ASAP.

Of course, my instincts also tell me to walk into her house, scoop her up, toss her onto her bed and claim her as my mate. Something I definitely can't do.

But one thing at a time.

"You bears behave yourself for Papa Deke," I say, remounting my bike.

"Sir, yessir!"

Excellent.

"Get in the van," Deke orders the bears, and they scramble to obey. Deke steps closer to me, looking thoughtful.

"This private mission," he asks. "Is there anything I can do to help?"

It's normal for members of my pack to accept solo missions between bigger jobs. Usually small time stuff, like a bodyguard job or surveillance. Our alpha is fine with it as long as we clear it with him first.

"I'm all good," I tell him. "I'll radio for support if I need it."

"You do that." He pauses.

"Aww, Deke. Are we having a moment? Because I feel like we're having a moment." I put my hand on his shoulder and make a moon face.

"No," he swats me away, but he can't negate the fact that he took a moment to let me know he'd have my back.

"I hear you. Good luck dropping off the package." I wink. "Remember, you can't kill them." I point a finger gun at him, "but you could choke them out if they get too annoying." I wrap my fingers around my own neck. "Unconscious is technically alive. Babysitting rule number one–keep the kids alive."

Deke grunts.

"See? It's a good thing you're the one taking them back and not me."

I go to start my bike, and Deke grips my bike handle.

"One more thing. Call me Papa Deke again, and I'll gut you like a deer and dry you in strips."

I grin, showing all my teeth. "10-4... *Daddy.*"

Deke snarls, and I turn my bike around, shooting back out of Deke's reach, flashing him my megawatt smile before speeding off in a spray of gravel.

Down the road and out of Deke's view, I set a course for Julia's house, and relief washes through me. My wolf wants to stay close to her side. Her son—-my nephew—is thirteen. Puberty is a tough time for any kid but more so for a shifter.

With Geo's wolf surfacing, things can get out of control. My brother guided me through my first shifts. It was rough.

If anything happens to me...

I promised my brother I'd look out for his family. For ten years, I've sent money. I've watched over them from afar—checking in on them from my lookout post on the hill or through the cameras I secretly installed in the tall pines over their house.

But to guide Geo through his shifts, I'll have to show up. In person.

That means being with Julia. In person. In close quarters, like those few years I stayed with them, when Geo was just a tot. Before Geoffrey died.

Geo's wolf will need my presence. I may be a general fuck-up compared to the guys on my team, but I'm all he's got.

I'll keep my head down, my sights focused on helping Geo through his first shifts. Make sure he's got a handle on his animal. I'll help him and his mom as best I can.

And whatever I do, I won't give into instinct and touch, taste or claim Julia.

The human I shouldn't want so badly.

* * *

Julia

The morning alarm always comes too soon. I roll over and smack the ringing clock hard enough to knock it off the bedside table. I'm old school—I still use an alarm clock. I don't sleep with my cell phone by the bed because if I did, I'd look at it first thing in the morning, and then my work day would begin the moment I woke up.

I've never been a morning person, but I have work to do, and getting Geo off to school these days is harder than ever.

I shower, dress in my work-from-home outfit of comfy leggings and a nice blouse, and head downstairs, rapping on Geo's door as I pass.

"Morning," I call. "Time for school." I knock again and wait until I hear a muffled groan confirming that he heard me. Resisting the urge to barge in and make sure he starts his morning routine, I force myself to go downstairs. I keep an ear out while I make coffee, hoping to hear him head to the shower.

I'm trying to give him his privacy and space. But it's hard, so much harder than I thought it would be.

There's a picture of our family—me, Geo and his late father Geoffrey—on the fridge. It's the last photo we took together. Geo was three, and his sweet little face makes my heart catch. He's the perfect blend of me and his father. He got silky dark hair and a golden brown tint to his skin from my side, but his face structure is all his father's. And somehow he inherited Geoffrey's striking green eyes, eyes that glow bright when their wolf side is close to taking over.

The first time Geo's eyes caught the light and flashed like Geoffrey's used to, I froze like a rabbit. I had to excuse myself before Geo could scent my freak out. I'd almost forgotten I was a human raising a shifter, a shifter who one day would be able to turn into a giant wolf. *And then what will I do?* I never thought I'd have to face this moment alone, without Geoffrey here to guide him.

I almost dialed the number Geoffrey's brother gave me in case of emergencies. Almost. It's been ten years since Channing joined the Army. I thought we'd see him between tours, on holidays, but he literally hasn't been back since.

Geo wouldn't even recognize his uncle if he saw him on the street. But I get it. He's in some kind of special ops in the military. Probably hasn't been in the country in years. Still, it would've been nice to hear from him. A letter. A text. A Christmas gift for his nephew. Of course, shifters don't celebrate Christmas, so maybe that was expecting too much. But how about Halloween?

But, no. Nothing. No contact besides the money that magically appears in envelopes. Which I appreciate, but money isn't really my love language. So, I've had to figure everything out myself. But it's fine. Geo and I have done just fine on our own. We're our own unit.

Before my coffee finishes brewing, Geo's door creaks open, and he stomps down the hall. I hold my breath until the shower upstairs turns on.

Maybe this morning won't be a struggle.

My phone buzzes with incoming emails and texts. I unplug it from the kitchen outlet and start scrolling through the messages at the same time I open the fridge and pull out eggs and milk. And bacon. Shifters need meat. That's what Geoffrey used to tell me. He could down five hamburgers in a single sitting. And that was on a resting day.

My assistant has already sent over five emails. Rather than take the time to reply to each one of them, I dial her office while I set the frying pan on the stovetop and start cracking eggs.

"Hi Kelly, it's me. I got your messages. Thought it would be easier to call." I go through her questions while I beat a half dozen eggs for a scramble and put the bacon in the broiler.

It's sizzling when Geo thumps down the stairs.

I end the call. "Morning," I chirp, turning to Geo with a smile. "I made you bacon."

He doesn't answer but looks less grumpy than usual. His hair sticks up in adorable spikes, and it takes everything in me not to cross the room and run my hand over his head like I used to.

"Is your iPad charged for school?" I ask. His school issued every kid a tablet at the beginning of the year. Something about being a STEM school. I hate it because it means Geoffrey doesn't have to learn to spell or type on a keyboard. Autocorrect and voice-to-text are his best friends.

"Yeah," he grunts.

"Fill your water bottle, please."

He slouches to his backpack to pull out the water bottle and fill it.

"I'm glad you showered." There, some positive reinforcement. "Did you put on deodorant?"

He sniffs his shirt like he's checking. For a kid with such a sensitive sense of smell, you'd think he'd notice his own increased body odors.

"Geo..." I don't want to nag. He gets so defensive as if I'm criticizing his new body and its smells rather than trying to make sure he takes care of basic hygiene.

With a grunt, he turns and stomps back up the stairs. He's so touchy about smells I had to buy five different brands

Alpha's Command

of deodorant before I found him one he didn't hate. It's a natural one with a cedar and sandalwood scent.

When did my sweet boy turn into a stinky, grouchy teen? It was so much easier when I could tickle him out of his bad moods. Now, tickling rarely works, and the last time I tried, I was shocked by how long his limbs were—I nearly got kicked.

I bustle around the kitchen, making him a plate of food and setting it on the table.

"Breakfast is ready," I call up the stairs and bite my tongue before I nag him to get it while it's hot. Thinking of a task I forgot to ask Kelly about, I dial her back as I busy myself with wiping down counters and emptying the dishwasher. It's usually Geo's job, but if he does it now, he'll be late for school. At least he took out the trash. He didn't put a new trash bag in the bin, but it's a start.

A cold draft leaks in from the front of the house, and when I check it, I find the front door has cracked open.

"Okay, that was it. I need to get Geo out the door, but I'll be available in a half hour," I promise Kelly, ending the call while staring at the open door. I gasp and grasp the handle. I know I locked it and threw the deadbolt last night. Did Geo go out?

In the street, it looks like something knocked over the trash bin. Trash is strewn into the street. I grab a coat and hustle out to clean the mess up.

Geo must have forgotten to close the lid, and an enterprising raccoon took advantage. A chicken carcass from last night's dinner is strewn across the pavement. I grab a ripped-up cloth and use it to pick up the smellier bits of trash.

I'm almost done when I realize what I'm clutching. The

ripped-up cloth is a t-shirt. And not just any t-shirt, but a band t-shirt. The front reads *Faust* and has a picture of Luna, the lead singer, howling into the microphone.

Faust is Geo's favorite band, and he treasures each piece of memorabilia like a dragon hoarding his treasure. There's no way he'd throw this shirt away, but here it is stuffed into the trash can. He wore this shirt last night, and now it's torn to shreds like a wild animal got a hold of it. There are dull red smears on the faded fabric.

And it hits me. I know what happened last night. Why the door was open and why this shirt is torn. I grip the shirt so hard my knuckles go white.

"Oh God, it's happening." I've half-hoped for, half-dreaded this day would come. That Geo's shifter genes would surface, and he'd become a wolf like his father.

It's time to have *the talk*.

Well, we've already had the first talk. I reminded him when he first got underarm hair and his voice started cracking that he may shift. It seemed he'd forgotten over the years. He knows he's different. That he's much stronger and heals faster than his classmates. That it's imperative he hides that from all humans. But we haven't talked about shifting in years. I didn't bring it up because...well, I wasn't even sure if he'd become a wolf. He's half-human, half-shifter. Geoffrey told me sometimes half-breeds can't shift. I didn't want to get Geo's hopes up that he'd have some kind of superpower only for him to be disappointed.

But I also didn't want him to be taken by surprise if he *did* end up having the ability to shapeshift. So we'd talked once, and then I never brought it up again.

But now, it seems it's happening. Geo's shifter genes were strong enough. He's a wolf, like his father.

And I have absolutely no idea how to help him through this life change.

I head back inside, my coffee sloshing in my stomach. When I reach the front door, I get another nasty surprise. There are claw marks on the faded wood, down at the bottom. The bronze doorknob is crushed, which is impossible. Unless... someone unnaturally strong gripped it hard and broke it. Someone who didn't know his own strength.

Geo is at the table, scarfing down his breakfast, barely chewing each mouthful. Geoffrey ate like that, especially after a shift.

"*Mijo.*" I approach him slowly. "Last night, did you..." How do I say this?

Geo looks up and blanches when he sees the torn shirt I'm holding. His expression shutters. "I don't want to talk about it."

"Sweetie." I sink down into a chair next to him. "It's normal. It's nothing to be ashamed of."

"I said, *I don't want to talk about it.*" He shoves away from the table and stomps off to the living room.

"We need to talk about it." I follow him. "Did you leave the house during the night?"

He's at the door, putting on his coat. He mumbles something.

"What was that?"

"You know I did," he says loudly, his eyes flashing bright green.

"What happened to your shirt?" I hold up the torn cloth. "Did you get in a fight? Is this your blood?"

"No. I...hunted." He mutters the last word.

I force myself to swallow past the tight band around my throat. "You were a wolf."

He ducks his head, looking away. He tried to hide this from me—does he not want me to know? Does he think I'm ashamed of him? I'm messing this up.

I set the shirt down on a side table and try again. "Geo, it's normal for a boy—a shifter—your age to start to shift. Your father and I hoped you would inherit his genes. This is a good thing."

He ignores me, swinging on his backpack.

"I think we should talk about this."

"Mom, no. I'm going to be late." He opens the front door and slips out.

I'm not a shifter. How do I even begin to help Geo navigate puberty?

While I was pregnant, Geoffrey and I talked about our son possibly having shifter genes, but the adolescent onset of his shifter powers was so far away. Discussing the future and facing reality are two different things.

And it's not like there are parenting books I can read. *How to train your shifter animal. Seven steps to easy shifting.*

Geo was out last night. He turned into a wolf, tore his shirt and somehow got blood on it. *At least it wasn't his blood.*

He's only thirteen. He can't be running around at night. As a wolf. What if someone saw him?

God, this is a nightmare. I don't even know how to keep

Alpha's Command

my son safe. How to make him stay in the house all night. Whether he'll come home covered in animal blood. Or worse—not come home at all.

There are hunters out there who might shoot a wolf for sport. For a trophy head.

I shudder.

I throw open the door. Geo is striding down the driveway.

"Geoffrey, come back here."

"Don't call me that," he snaps without turning around. "That's not my name."

"Don't talk to your mother like that," a deep voice rumbles, and both Geo and I turn towards the interruption.

A motorcycle's parked fifty feet away, on the other end of the quiet cul-de-sac. If it was there a few minutes ago, I didn't notice it. Beside the bike slouches a tall man in baggy sweatpants and a brown leather jacket. He crosses the cul-de-sac and heads up our drive. The sun peeks out from behind a cloud. The light hits his blond, buzz cut hair, and for a second, he looks so like my late husband, it takes my breath away. Then he angles his head and a dimple appears on either cheek. "Hey, Julia."

Geo's gone tense at my side. "Who are you?" He steps in front me protectively, even though he's only an inch taller than I am. "How do you know my mom?"

"It's okay, Geo." I put a hand on my son's vibrating arm. "I know him. This is your Uncle Channing."

Chapter Three

Julia

"I don't have an uncle," Geo says.

"Geo." Channing's voice is deeper than I remember. "It's been a few years."

"Ten." I can't keep the tightness out of my voice, and Geo tenses again. A low growl rumbles in his throat. Not a human growl.

That's his wolf.

I'm suddenly flooded with memories of his father's growl that surfaced any time Geoffrey thought I was in danger.

Oh my God. I need to stay calm, so Geo does too. If he thinks Channing's a threat, there's no telling what he'll do.

"It's been *ten years* since we've seen you," I say to Channing, proud of how I keep my voice level.

Where have you been?

"I know," he says. "I'm sorry. I sent money."

Unbelievable. "All those envelopes were from you?"

He nods.

"Okay." I pin him with a look that says *I'll deal with you later*.

Channing's green eyes sparkle in the morning light. He's taller than I remember, his shoulders broader. Or maybe it's how he's holding himself. His easy posture can't hide the powerful muscles under his motorcycle jacket. He's filled out since he was nineteen, which seems surprising because he was already built of honed muscle then.

He's wearing a brown leather bomber and nothing else. No shirt. The jacket's unzipped, giving me a clear view of his sculpted pectoral muscles, his spectacularly ripped abs. He's got more than a six pack hiding under his unfortunate outfit.

Not that I'm looking. That would be weird.

I tear my eyes away. "Geo, you've got to go. You'll miss the bus."

"I don't want to leave you alone with him," Geo says.

"He's fine," I say to Geo at the same time Channing hitches a thumb behind him, making his jacket flap open further, revealing a toned, taut chest that would make a model jealous. "Ever been on a motorcycle? I can give you a ride—"

"Absolutely not," I snap. I know my son has exceptional healing abilities, but I also know motorcycles are death-rides. I also know shifters aren't as indestructible as they believe. I learned that in the worst possible way.

Geo squints at the bike, studying it.

"You sure?" Channing grins, flashing his deep dimples. "It'd be a chance for us to get to know each other."

"No." I draw myself up to my full height, which is about a foot shorter than Channing. "No motorcycles."

Channing's grin falls away. He regards me, looking thoughtful. I've never seen him look so serious. So grown up. "All right. Geo, you heard your mom. Time to get to school."

I grit my teeth. *How dare you tell my kid what to do?* I press down my indignation so Geo doesn't pick it up in my posture and my scent.

Geo doesn't think anything of it. He shrugs on his backpack and heads down the drive. I wait until my son's out of sight and put my hands on my hips. Channing's still watching Geo, his expression distant.

His face is harder than I remember, honed to perfection. He's still got the dimples—he shows them off when he's turning on the charm. His ears used to stick out, looking too big for his head. Not anymore. Not even with his buzz cut. He's got the body and bone structure of a movie star.

Not that I think he's attractive. He's way too young for me. And he's my brother-in-law. I'm just noticing the differences.

As soon as Geo's out of earshot, I clear my throat to get his attention. "It's not your place to give Geo directives. You can't show up after ten years and pretend you have a role in his life."

"I apologize." The sharp green gaze lands on my face. There's something oddly intimate about the way he studies me. It's disconcerting.

I summon my anger. "What are you doing here?"

Whenever Channing did something dumb or got in trouble, he used to cock his head to the side and put on an *aw shucks* expression. A get-out-of-jail free card that worked on everyone but his older brother.

He does an improved version of this move, tilting his head, so his stunning eyes flash and pair with a hint of dimple. "I can't visit my favorite nephew?"

I steel myself against his charm. "He's your *only* nephew. Not like you care."

The dimples fall away. "Of course I care, Julia." I'm surprised at how genuinely hurt he seems by my remark.

"Really?" I cross my arms over my chest and raise my brows. "Then where have you been? Are you even still in the military?"

"Here and there. Everywhere." He shrugs. "I left the military a few years ago for private security work. I sent you a text."

"From a burner phone. *In case of emergencies,* you said. As if that was enough explanation."

God, I wonder if he's into something illegal? Followed in his dead-beat dad's footsteps. He got himself into a lot of trouble as a teen, which is why Geoffrey had him move to Arizona with us when he was seventeen, rather than stay in Kentucky with their dad's pack. Those wolves were trouble.

Even when he was with us, he was never home. He ran wild—out all night. Racing motorbikes. Then cars. And he was a ladies' man from a young age.

He lifts those muscled shoulders in a casual shrug, like his activities of the past ten years don't matter. He was never the responsible one in the family. Geoffrey was.

Channing's gaze narrows on my hands. "Why do you smell like rabbit blood?"

I glance down at my silk blouse, checking for stains.

Nothing. The scent from Geo's kill must be on my hands. Shifters have a powerful sense of smell.

"It's nothing," I say.

"That's a lie, Julia." He takes a step forward, and now he's close enough to touch. His eyes flash a brighter, inhuman green, and I shiver. His wolf has the same color eyes as Geo's. As Geoffrey's. "Did Geo bring home a kill?"

"That's none of your business."

"It's exactly my business. That's why I'm here. To guide Geo through his shifter puberty."

Oh.

I should be glad. This is exactly what I need. Except, seeing Channing in person after so many years brings back a truckload of hurt. I'm struck by the full force of how much I missed him. How disappointed I've been over the years that he never came back. He lived with us for a couple of years. I thought he'd stay a part of our family after Geoffrey's death, but he totally and completely bailed.

"That won't be necessary," I say.

"I disagree. And I think I get to make this call since I'm the shifter and you're not."

"I beg your pardon," I snap.

"Denied." He winks and steps past me, heading towards my porch.

For a second, I stand, mouth open, in my driveway. *Did he just walk away from me?* If my head could explode, it would.

I whirl and chase him up the steps, ready to give him a piece of my mind.

Channing's frowning at my front door.

"Did Geo do that?" He points to the crumpled doorknob.

I swallow my annoyance. Whatever's going on with Geo takes precedence. "I think so. I don't know."

"What about these?" He squats and points to scratches on the door and door frame. They're down by the sill. I wouldn't have noticed them if Channing hadn't pointed them out, but now that he has, they look like a cross between a big dog and a mountain lion swiped at the door, gouging the old wood.

"I guess. He wouldn't tell me what happened." My shoulders slump. This whole morning is a bust. I want to go back to bed. Rewind time, go back to when Geo was a toddler. When Geoffrey was alive and life was simpler.

Channing walks into my house like he owns it and picks up Geo's torn band shirt. He lowers his head and sniffs it. His eyes flash.

"Definitely a rabbit," he announces. "How many times has he shifted?" He ponders the shredded fabric.

"I-I honestly don't know. I found the front door ajar and the shirt in shreds this morning. He didn't want to talk about it."

"It probably scared him. Looks like it caught him unaware," he says. "He felt the need to go outside, maybe kicked off his shoes and jeans. But the shift came faster than he expected. He was still wearing his shirt." He holds the t-shirt up, showing me the way the fabric is stretched out, split at the collar. "Once he was in wolf form, he didn't stop to shake it off. He scented a rabbit and went for it. Caught it too." Channing looks pleased.

I struggle to assimilate this information. Even though I'd

guessed it was something like that, Channing's confirmation makes it all the more real. "My son is a shifter who doesn't know what's happening to him or how to control it."

Channing nods.

All sorts of images fly through my head. Geo sneaking out of the house, into the forest. Turning into a wolf. Running through the trees, scenting wild animals, hunting them, killing them...

"He can't go hunting alone in the middle of the night." My voice pitches up with panic. "I'm not okay with this."

"It's all right," Channing soothes, reaching for my arms and rubbing them. "That's why I'm here. He needs me."

His touch discombulates me. He's my brother-in-law. My *much younger* brother-in-law. And this feels...a little too intimate.

Not his touch. My reaction to it.

Because I'm not seeing Channing as a boy anymore. Channing is all man.

Well, technically not all *man* because he's a shifter, but *all male*.

I nod and take a step back, out of his grasp. "This is crazy. I wish he would've come to me."

"He probably didn't want to bother you. And he wasn't thinking as a human. He was thinking as a shifter. A wolf. The animal is more straightforward about things. He needed to be in the woods, so he went. He wanted to hunt, so he did. This property is perfect for it."

"That's what Geoffrey said when we toured it with the realtor," I say on autopilot. "And about five years ago, someone bought up the rest of the lots around our house.

They were supposed to develop them, but they haven't, so the cul de sac is pretty private."

"Nice," Channing says.

I turn away, rubbing my temples. My mind is a tornado of thoughts, spinning around the image of my Geo, scared and alone. Turning into a wolf without knowing or understanding how it works. So much more intense than my puberty surprises of getting my period for the first time or growing hair in places it hadn't been before.

I sink onto the couch. "He's thirteen."

"He's at the right age for it."

What if he went too far and couldn't find his way home? What if a hunter found him? Would he shift back? Is he able to shift back and forth at will? What if he went out alone and was hurt?

Geo's all I have. I lost Geoffrey. I can't lose him, too.

"Julia," Channing is calling. "Julia."

I blink up at him.

"Breathe," he chides me gently, and I suck in a breath.

"That's it." Channing sits on the couch beside me. The springs creak under his solid weight, and my cushion tilts me towards him. "Deep breaths. It'll be okay."

"He's just a kid. He's too young. He can't be out there alone." My chest feels tight. That's where my anxiety builds up, under my breastbone. If I were alone, I'd rub it away.

Channing stretches an arm behind me, resting it on the back of the couch. He's not touching me, but I'm enveloped in his warmth.

"I know. That's why I'm here," Channing says, his deep voice an ocean of calm. "This is perfectly normal."

My breathing eases. Channing's hand hovers over my shoulder, inches away, still not touching.

"He won't be alone. I'll be with him." Channing's eyes have dark rims and golden striations radiating out from the pupil. There's a bit of blond scruff on his chiseled cheeks.

He's so much bigger and broader than I am, taking up more than his share of space on the couch. In addition to the bomber jacket, he's wearing baggy sweatpants and black boots. And no shirt.

I wrinkle my nose. "Why aren't you wearing a shirt?"

He shrugs, his face doing the *aw, shucks* expression I know too well.

I straighten, scooting an inch to the left, away from him. He probably left his shirt in some poor woman's bed. I remember he was quite the ladies' man when he was in high school.

He probably gave her a night to remember and snuck out before dawn. She's probably waking up now, realizing he's gone. At least he left the shirt, she'll think, picking it up to inhale his scent. It's the only memento she has of the god who rocked her world all night.

Why am I thinking of Channing in bed? That's just wrong.

I press my hands to my cheeks. My skin scorches my palms.

"Julia?" His gaze falls to the wedding band Geoffrey gave me.

I'm not sure why I'm still wearing it. At first, I wasn't ready to take it off. Then it was comforting, and I wore it as a shield. And as the years went by, it never came off.

I fly off the couch, crossing the room. I'm warm all over. Is this a hot flash? It's gotta be a hot flash. "You need to go." I need to get control. This, whatever this is, needs to stop. "Now."

"Julia." The soft command in his voice makes me turn. He's risen from the couch, and the whole room seems smaller. "I'm not leaving."

"Well, that's a change."

His face hardens, and I know the blow landed. It hurts to hurt him, but I'll bring out the big guns if I have to. If that's what it takes him to leave.

Because I'm not sure he's the kind of role model I want for Geo. He may be a shifter, but he's wild and reckless. He showed up here without a shirt and on a motorcycle. Who does that? And why? This guy is not mentor material. Besides, seeing him is sort of painful. It reminds me of better times.

Of Geoffrey. Of how lonely I am now.

"I fucked up," he says. "I know that. If I could go back in time, I'd do it differently. But I'm here now, and I'm going to be here for Geo. And for you." He steps close, into my space. His eyes roam over my face.

I don't know why he added that last part—*And for you.*

I don't need anything from him.

I definitely don't want to take him up on it.

What do I look like to him? He's changed so much, but I've changed, too. Is he noticing how much older I look? All the wrinkles I have? Am I still even attractive to a male anymore?

My spine turns to steel. "This conversation is over. I need to get to work."

For a second, he stands there, looming over me. He's a foot taller and has a hundred pounds more muscle than me packed onto his taut frame. Maybe two hundred pounds.

There's no way I can throw him out. He could pick me up with one hand. Or carry me in a fireman's hold wherever he wanted to go. If I complained, he'd smack my ass. Flip me down, gag me, tie me up. He probably learned all sorts of moves and ways of restraining the enemy in the military.

Um...wow. Why am I thinking about Channing that way?

My body quivers. I stiffen to get it under control.

One of Channing's brows quirks. He takes a thoughtful inhale of my scent.

I clear my throat and raise my chin.

"I'll let you work, but this isn't over." Channing heads for the door but pauses with his hand on the frame. "Geoffrey told me to look after his family. That's what I'm going to do."

A scoff flies from my throat. Too little, too late. "We did just fine for over a decade. We don't need you."

He opens his mouth to say something.

"Close the door on your way out."

With one last lingering look, he does. I slump against the wall. I'm shaking, sweat lining my back.

He's gone.

That's good.

I should feel relieved. Instead, a sense of unease crawls up my spine. I totally misplayed that. Channing is literally the only person I know who can help me and guide Geo right now. Driving him away was probably not my best move.

I may have screwed up.

* * *

Channing

She's as beautiful as ever. Silky dark hair, dark eyes flashing fire. When I got close to Geo, I thought she was going to bare her teeth and snarl at me like a momma wolf.

Seeing them up close and in human form isn't the same as watching them on a camera or lurking behind their house as a wolf. Geo's bigger, taller, his baby fat melted away. His voice is deeper. He's crossing the threshold between boy and man.

He looks so much like my brother, it's a fist in the gut.

And Julia... Julia is everything. All I ever wanted. All I've thought of for these past ten years. Her oval face and slender, toned body. Her scent–more complex up close–is a revelation. All the feelings I've suppressed rise like a phoenix, scorching my insides with fire. There's nothing left of me and my defenses.

It's dangerous to get so close. But I'm used to danger. I have to bear it, for Geo's sake. This will be the hardest mission I've ever taken on.

Julia thinks she's won this round. I lope down the driveway, listening to her moving in her home. I hate to leave her, but I need supplies.

I have a burner phone, but I'll have to stop to buy clothes. Time to call in every favor I have.

I've got work to do. A family to protect. To reclaim.

We did just fine for over a decade. We don't need you.

When my brother died, I was nineteen. A man-child. Selfish and irresponsible. That's the Channing Julia knows. She blames me for going AWOL, and I understand. She sees it as more proof of my selfishness. She doesn't know, and I don't know how to explain why I had to leave then.

But then, having her pissed off and thinking the worst of me is probably for the best. She's my brother's mate. Not mine to claim, no matter how much my wolf may want her.

Chapter Four

Julia

After the events of this morning, it's a miracle that I make my first Zoom meeting—a contract review—on time. I moved to Flag right after law school to provide legal counsel for a non-profit on indigenous water rights protection, and I worked there for almost twelve years. They closed down last year, though, so I took a lucrative but less-fulfilling work-from-home position as private counsel for van den Berg.

When Geo's grown, I want to return to the non-profit sector, so I can make a difference in the community. Tweaking contracts for an eccentric billionaire isn't really life purpose stuff.

My heart is still jumping from my quarrel with Channing this morning. When Geoffrey was alive, he took on handling his brother. Channing was a mess, in trouble at school, disappearing on weekends and showing up for dinner with two fading black eyes and evidence of healing road rash on his bare back. Channing lost his shirt a lot back then, too. No dangerous activity was off limits. Fight clubs, back street bike races, climbing water towers for a midnight swim—it was a miracle Channing didn't do jail time. He always managed to wriggle out of any consequences with nothing but that dimpled smile.

Except with his brother.

Geoffrey always saw through the charm. He would pull Channing aside after dinner. Together they'd do the dishes and put up the food while Geoffrey lectured about responsibility and good behavior.

Watching these stern but gentle lectures was how I knew Geoffrey would be a good father.

But Channing...he couldn't seem to care about his own life or the mayhem he caused around him.

And now he's back, if stopping by for a fifteen-minute argument counts as back.

I focus on the work at hand. The contract review is for one of my boss's many companies. The counsel for the other company has a dry-as-dust voice that drones on and on. I look serious for the camera, pretend I'm listening and nod at appropriate times. Mostly, I keep one ear cocked for the sound of motorcycle pipes in my drive.

This isn't over.

Will he come back?

Do I want him to?

Channing could help Geo through his shifts. But any help from him might do more harm than good. I can only imagine the bad habits he'd teach Geo. Sneaking out of the house, running through the woods at all hours—Channing seemed to think this was all within the realm of normal behavior. Geo needs someone to teach him how to shift responsibly, not get in trouble. Channing wouldn't be a good influence.

And when it gets too hard, I'm sure he'll just bail. He's not the type to handle responsibility. I don't want Geo to get attached to him and then have his heart broken. Or worse, to see him as a role model and follow him into something reckless or dangerous.

I grip a pen so hard it cracks and spatters ink against my blouse. Luckily, I can adjust my computer, so my camera only shows my face, not my stained clothes. When my meeting ends, I change and brush my hair. Not for any reason. I'm definitely not thinking about having Channing in my house again.

Lord, it's been way too long since Geoffrey died. I should've gotten myself out there and dated. Maybe I'd have met someone by now. Then I wouldn't be so enervated over my dead husband's *much younger* brother showing up. What's wrong with me?

I stare in the mirror. I don't recognize the Julia looking back at me. Her cheeks are flushed like she's been day drinking. She looks half-wild.

More proof that Channing is a bad influence. Fifteen minutes in his presence affected me far more than it should have.

He said he wanted to help. To fulfill his promise to his brother.

How typical and absurd for Channing to show up, half-dressed, and pretend he's going to be Mr. Responsible. How dare he look so much like Geoffrey and Geo, the two people I love the most. How dare he look so damn hot?

Or maybe I'm just mad at myself for being attracted to him. I mean, that's just... crazy. I must be missing Geoffrey, and Channing is the closest thing I've seen to him.

But he's ten years younger than I am!

When my morning meetings end, I take my aggression out on a badly-written contract, ripping it to shreds with comments, clacking at my computer with enough force to break the keys. Not even my mid-morning yoga break calms my nerves.

Geo comes home in the middle of one of my afternoon meetings. By the time I can check on him, he's ensconced in his room, headphones on, doing his homework.

I've been so distracted, I forgot to plan dinner or call Geo's current school to get his transcript sent to the new private school he'll be attending, thanks to my boss. I blame Channing for this, too. A glance out the front windows shows an empty cul-de-sac.

My last meeting of the day is with my boss, Mr. van den Berg. A year ago, his main law firm hired me for some contract work. He was so pleased with my work, he created a full-time position for me. It pays well and works around my single mom schedule. It's mostly boring business and real estate contracts. Rich people tend to have all sorts of businesses and moving parts to hide their assets. And Mr. van den Berg is very, very rich.

At sixty-five, my boss is fit and tanned from his golf addiction, with a kindly grandfather face and a beard that's more white than gray. He joins the video conference a few minutes late, and the screen gives me a view of his grand mahogany desk and crystal decanter filled with the world's most expensive scotch. He raises his half-filled glass in a toast, his dark eyes twinkling.

"Hello, Mr. van den Berg. I hope I'm not interrupting something important," I joke because we had this meeting scheduled. It's no secret he has a standing four o'clock date with a glass of whisky.

"Not at all, not at all. You'll forgive me for my little indulgence." He sips his drink.

"Of course. Honestly, I need one of those." As soon as my work day is over, I'll pour myself a glass of wine.

My boss looks concerned. "Long day, Ms. Armstrong?"

"No, work is going well. I wish the rest of my life were as manageable."

"Ah." Mr. van den Berg sets down his glass with a clink. "I hope Geoffrey Jr. isn't giving you trouble. He is of that age."

"Yes, he is." I smile weakly.

"He's a good kid. Growing into a fine young man. I hope I don't overstep when I say I have a soft spot for you two."

"You've been more than generous." With my boss's help, I'm getting Geo into an exclusive private school, Woodman Prep. Tuition's expensive, but my new generous salary will cover it. More importantly, Mr. van den Berg's referral ensures Geo has a place. "I can't thank you enough for all you've done."

He waves a hand. "It was my pleasure. You've done a fine job as a mother, but a growing boy needs a good example. A challenge, more responsibility. A robust environment. He'll get all that at Woodman."

"You went there as a boy, correct?"

"Yes. Don't worry, the facilities are modernized. All new computers, tablets, and sports facilities."

It actually wasn't the STEM technology stuff that attracted me to Woodman. He gets plenty of that at his current school. It was the wide open campus and outdoor learning activities. "Geo is excited about the mountain biking class."

"Ah yes, that's what he needs, lots of exercise. Did the school receive my referral?"

"Yes, and we're so grateful—"

He waves off my gratitude. "Then everything's settled."

I nod, even though everything's not settled. I still have to organize the first payment and the transfer of Geo's transcript. It's all on my to do list.

"He's a fine boy," Mr. van den Berg says. "His father would be proud."

"Thank you for saying that."

The growl of an engine outside makes my head turn. My home office is in the unused third bedroom, facing the cul-de-sac. There's a bright red pickup truck rolling up to the house, towing an open trailer with a familiar-looking motorcycle.

I can't stop my frown.

"Everything all right?"

"Excuse me, Mr. van den Berg. Someone just pulled up to the house." The red truck pulls into my driveway, blocking my car.

"Uninvited company?"

"Something like that." I crane my neck. I can't see who jumped out of the red truck and slammed the door, but I can guess. "Geo's uncle is back in town."

"Uncle?" Mr. van den Berg's bushy brows knit together. "I didn't know he had an uncle."

"On his father's side. We haven't seen him in a few years."

"I see. Well, best not keep him waiting too long. Shall we?"

I get to work, focusing on running down the list of things my boss needs to review and making notes of his critiques and preferences. We end a few minutes early.

"I'll compile this and send over the documents for you to sign," I say.

"No rush. I won't check my email until tomorrow. Go see your guest."

"Thank you, sir." I log off, feeling guilty. Mr. van den Berg is so nice. I type up a quick draft of my notes anyway and schedule it to leave my inbox first thing in the morning. Then I stand and square my shoulders.

Time to rip Channing a new one.

The big red truck is still in my driveway. I can't see Channing, but there are tools spread out on a tarp half on, half off my lawn. There's a banging sound followed by the whine of a power tool.

What is he up to?

Geo's door is still shut. He's probably done with his homework by now and on to gaming. With his headphones on, he's in his own little world.

Which is good. He won't hear me unleashing the beast on his uncle.

Channing's crouched beside my half open front door. Once again, he is not wearing a shirt. Sweat glistens on the awesome muscles of his chest and back.

He looks up, and our eyes meet. Green and gold in dark rims. My steps falter, and I trip over a worn duffel bag in Army green.

"Careful," Channing warns, too late.

I stop and seethe, marshaling my thoughts. I kick the bag, but it's too heavy to send flying, so I slide it with my foot out of the way. "What are you doing here?"

"Fixing the knob. See?" He steps back and makes a show of turning the shiny new doorknob. "Now the door can shut properly."

He's right, the door's fixed. Something on my to do list that I would've gotten to, someday. Certainly not today.

I'll thank him after I murder him. *Why is his shirt off?* "Channing—"

"No, need to thank me," he says, before I can light into him. "You've got some shingles missing on your roof. I'm doing that next. And I ordered pizza for dinner. Hope that's okay."

I'm panting with irritation, but I can't keep up. Doorknob, shingles…pizza? "No!"

He tilts his head. "You don't like pizza? I also got hot wings."

"You can't just show up here and…" I wave my hands. I'm a lawyer. I use complex language all day. Channing has me at a complete loss for words. It might be his shirtlessness.

His chest is dusted with golden hairs that curl. I mean, I'm not looking at his chest hair, though. *I'm not!*

He straightens and takes a step towards me. The sunlight arching over his shoulder sets his toned body glowing. It's a sight to make a Vogue photographer swoon.

Stop perving on your baby brother-in-law! I'm losing my grip on my anger.

The light gilds his long lashes and brings out the gold in his eyes. "I told you this morning. You need me, Julia."

Ugh. I need him like I need a bullet in the head. Okay, maybe a slight exaggeration, but his cockiness is staggering. As if I should be happy he just suddenly decided to grace us with his presence and help with a few handyman tasks? I don't think so.

"No, I don't." I fold my arms over my chest, trying to stay resistant to the Channing charm. And his eight pack. It's hard when the golden hairs on his chest glow in the sunset. When I'm literally having a *Magic Mike* moment with him on my front porch.

"I don't," I insist again, but I sound like I'm convincing myself. "I told you to leave."

"I did leave. And then I came back."

"I meant for you to leave permanently." I've taken a few steps forward, and Channing and I are inches apart. The heat from his body vibrates between us. He smells like the outdoors, fresh and wild. A bead of sweat rolls down the center of his chest, following the groove and contours of his muscles. And I'm pissed that I notice.

"Not going to happen, Jewels."

The old nickname sparks a sense of longing–for the past.

When I had Geoffrey. When Channing was the loveable, wild young man living with us. He used to purposely spell Jules like a Jewel to be cute.

But the longing morphs into something different. Not for the past—for something else. Like I want Channing to fill the void Geoffrey left. But that's wrong. Besides, Channing can't be relied upon.

"I don't need you," I assert, even though it's a lie. "We don't need you."

Channing leans back and takes me in, all five feet, one inch of irritation. "You're lying." He taps his nose. "I can smell it. You've needed me for a long time."

"Maybe a decade ago. But certainly not now." I'm not going to back down. Lawyers never back down.

"Then and now." He sounds contrite. "I have a lot to make up for." He backs away, going back to the door and packing away his tools.

"You can't... you don't... there's no making up anything. I told you to get out. This is my home."

"And Geo's. You gonna ask him?"

"He wants nothing to do with you, either."

"He doesn't know me. And he needs me right now."

"And who's fault is that?"

"Mine. It's mine, Julia. It's all my fault. And I'm sorry."

His apology leaves me breathless. Channing never apologized for the dumb things he did. Maybe he has grown up a bit.

"You can't just show up and say you're going to make it right."

Alpha's Command

"I know. I'm going to prove myself to you. You say you don't need me, but you do need a handyman."

I fold my arms over my chest. "I have a handyman."

"Then what's with the shingles?" He backs out of the house and down the steps to squint at the roof. I should shut the door in his face and lock it, but that would hardly stop Channing. He's been picking locks since he was a teen.

So I follow him outside to look up at the roof, which I hadn't even realized needed help.

"You have a few more years before you have to replace this," he says. "But not if you don't get the shingles replaced. There might already be water damage."

Ah. Well, that explained it.

I grit my teeth. "I called a roofer a couple years ago. He did two days of work that I paid him for and never showed up again."

Channing's eyes flash. "What's his name?"

"Why?"

He folds his arms over his chest, making his biceps bulge even bigger. I try not to stare at them. *God*, they're big. "Gonna have a chat with him."

"It doesn't matter. I can get a new roofer. It's on the to-do list."

"What else is on the to-do list?"

"None of your business."

"Wrong. It is my business. I'm making it mine."

"I'm going to get to it," I insist. I hate that I feel the need to explain myself to him, but I do. "Hiring people takes time. And money."

"What happened to the money I sent you?"

"The envelopes of cash? I use it for groceries, restaurants, things like that."

"That's it? Julia, it's hundreds of thousands of dollars..."

"I know," I snap. "And I didn't know how it was obtained or whether it was legal. I don't know how to spend it. I can't walk into a bank and say, "Here's a sack full of cash, please pay off my mortgage."

"Why not?"

"Because it isn't done!" I throw up my hands. "Normal people don't carry around sacks full of unmarked bills. I'd look like I run a cartel."

Channing grunts. "I didn't think of that."

"Of course not. Because you *don't think*."

"I'm used to getting paid in cash. And yes, it was legal. I told you, I work in the private sector now. It's high-risk work, which makes it lucrative. But you're right, not everyone is used to dealing with stacks of cash. But enough are. Take this truck." He tosses a thumb behind him. "The guy who sold me the trailer had it sitting on his lot. Told him I wanted to buy it, he said to name a price."

"You bought that today?"

"After my errands. That's why it took me a while to get back here."

"That's...not how you buy a truck. What about the vehicular history? The accident report? The pink slip?"

He shrugs, and the movement makes every one of his muscles stand out in relief. He's got more than his fair share. An eight pack of abs with a ladder of smaller muscles up his sides and a sleek v leading to the waistband of his sweatpants.

Alpha's Command

Holy...I tear my eyes away from them.

"It'll work out. You worry too much. Have you taught Geo to drive?" He stoops to grab his tool kit.

My eyes bug out of my head. "What? Of course not. He's thirteen."

"Well, there you go. I can teach him."

"He's too young!"

"He'll need to practice before he gets his permit. We can go off road."

"Absolutely not," I grind out. "You can use the truck to go away."

"Denied." He flashes the dimples with the wink. Enough to make a lesser woman's knees go weak. I hold strong. Well, I try to.

Channing sets his tool kit back in the truck and turns to me. His dimples don't make an appearance, but they're hovering just out of sight. Does my irritation amuse him?

I'm normally cool, calm and collected. I debate for a living. I just need to lay out my argument, make my case. But Channing looks ready for a photoshoot, leaning against his truck like that. It's discombobulating. Plus, there's the fact that he resembles Geoffrey. That must be it. I'm just thrown off by seeing someone who looks so similar to the love of my life.

"You bought a truck but didn't think to buy a shirt?"

As soon as the words are out of my mouth, I know they're a mistake. The dimples appear.

"I bought a shirt. See?" There's a white t-shirt slung over the open window of his new truck. He picks it up and tugs it over his torso. The soft fabric molds lovingly to his form. It's two sizes too small.

He spreads his hands. "Better?" He looks like a cologne model in GQ Magazine. Covering up his chest doesn't change his appeal.

The veins and sleek strength of his forearms are enough to do it for me. Not to mention his hands.

Oh God, his hands.

I avert my eyes and pretend to frown at the door.

"You didn't have to fix this."

"Yes, I did. And I'm replacing the old security system. State of the art."

"We don't have a security system."

"Yeah, you did."

I open my mouth to argue, but the squeal of tire wheels cuts me off. A battered Honda Civic with a Pizza sign on its roof screeches into the cul-de-sac. A greasy-haired teen hops out, his arms full of a red delivery bag. "Pizza delivery?"

"Yep. I got it." Channing takes the five boxes and balances them on the truck bed while he pulls out his wallet. "Here ya go." He hands the delivery kid two hundred-dollar bills.

"Thanks, man!" The kid takes off.

"See? Cash." He waves his wallet. "It's easy. Soup's on!" He takes the pizza boxes and saunters past me, right into my house.

* * *

Channing

Alpha's Command

I set the pizzas out on the kitchen table, flipping up the tops to check which pizza is which. I inhale the scent of pepperoni and sausage, mostly to drive out the lavender and lilac scent that's driving me mad. My dick is so hard, I can barely stand upright. I will it to deflate, but it's an impossible task with Julia around. Any second now, she'll burst into the kitchen and tear me a new one. Not that I don't deserve it. That could be fun, too.

Today's gone better than I imagined it would. I can't win an argument with her, so I keep changing the subject to keep her guessing. Lay out the way it's going to be versus try to get her permission. She'll never give it. I have to convince her.

It doesn't help that every time she opens her mouth, I want to toss her over my shoulder like a caveman, kick down her bedroom door and claim her. If she knew the X-rated images charging through my head, she'd run away screaming. And that will get us nowhere.

First, family dinner. Then a chat with Geo. I'm here for Geo. I've got to help Geo. Those scratches he put on the door were no joke. Was he stuck in animal form for a while, frustrated and scared, not knowing how to shift back to human? How to get back inside his own house?

The thought is a dash of cold water on my libido. This is a mission, I need to treat it that way. It's not a chance to reconnect with Julia and make her understand why I kept my distance all these years.

Certainly not a chance to live out my every fantasy.

For years, I've been jerking off to the thought of Julia.

Threesomes, sexy MILFs, porn–I tried everything to get her out of my mind. I once left an orgy to jerk off in the bathroom. I closed my eyes and imagined Julia. Her dark eyes, her plump lips, her oval shaped face. It's the only thing that gets me off.

I thought I might have grown out of it over the years. Find my own mate instead of perving on my brother's. But now that I'm in her presence again, I realize that's not going to happen.

The real life version of Julia is enough to bring me to my knees.

Fates, I have to get myself under control. Too bad my wolf thinks all this arguing is foreplay.

The front door slams, and I brace myself.

Julia strides into the kitchen. Two bright spots unfurled on the crest of her cheeks. She's practically breathing steam, like a bull. Hot damn.

I turn to hide my grin and my chub, grabbing plates from the dishwasher. She stops short, staring at me like she doesn't recognize me. I set the table and continue unloading the dishwasher, keeping it between me and her in case she lunges at me.

Time to initiate my basic battle maneuvers: deflect, distract, dance around the wolf in the room. "I got five pizzas. Hope that's enough."

She chokes. "You think?" Sarcasm, nice.

"One and a half for Geo." I point to the piles. "Two for me. Will you eat more than a half?"

"No." I can hear her teeth grinding from here.

"I got you the eggplant parmesan pizza with extra basil. Is that still your favorite?"

Alpha's Command

She blinks. Once again, I've stunned her to speechlessness. And all because of a basic act of courtesy.

I was an asshole when I was younger. My brother moved me out here to live with him after he found out I was failing out of school back home. Geoffrey was responsible, a natural alpha, right from birth. I was the opposite. Not mean or bad on purpose, just a complete fuck-up.

Julia is a good girl. I'm sure she was an A student all through law school. Never stayed out late or partied too hard. Forget drag racing, she probably never drove above the speed limit. I doubt she's skinny dipped under the full moon. My behavior always horrified her.

"If we have leftovers, I figured we could have them for breakfast. Cold pizza for breakfast is my favorite."

She sputters. "That's not...we're not... "

I'm getting the sense that cold pizza is not an appropriate breakfast food in Julia's world. "Or I can make eggs," I offer. "I'm not a great cook, but it's hard to fuck up eggs."

"Language," she snarls.

"Sorry. Cock up? Mess up?" Shit, how do I talk without the F-word?

She's still sputtering. I open a drawer and sort the silverware. "You didn't change the kitchen layout," I remark, catching her off guard again. "I know where everything is. Sorry if I overstepped with the pizza. My point was, you don't have to feed me. And I can sleep on the floor. I've got my kit." I jerked my chin towards the front room where my duffel bag sits.

"You're not... you can't.... I'm not letting you stay here."

Time for the big guns. I reach over to the wine rack and

pull out a bottle of red. "Cabernet Sauvignon," I read, probably butchering the French. "You like a glass with dinner, right?" I pop the cork and find a wine glass. I pour it and advance, holding the glass out like a peace offering. She might hit me, but she won't risk spilling the wine.

I hope.

With an effort, she takes the glass and sets it on the table then turns to me. "What part of *leave us alone* do you not understand?" Her voice is low and dangerous.

I close the dishwasher and step to the table, resting my hands on the back of a chair. She has the same worn oak dining set that Geoffrey bought at a yardsale when I moved in. "Julia." My voice is low and patient. "You need to accept that I'm staying for a bit. I'm gonna help Geo–"

"No." She holds up a hand, but I continue, "--and fix your house and do whatever else needs doing on your to do list. Replace the shingles, upgrade the security system..."

"We don't have a security system," she says.

Time to come clean. "Yeah you do. I installed it when you took Geo to Disneyland."

Her brows knot. "That was years ago."

"Yep. Right after I got back from a tour. I wanted eyes on the house."

"Are you telling me that you had cameras installed in my house?"

I nod.

Her nostrils flare. If she were a dragon, she'd be breathing fire. "Where?"

"All over. I had to keep an eye on you while I was gone on missions. Before that, I hired a friend to check on you. You might've seen him from time to time. Big guy, drove an old Charger."

She blinks. "The Charger with a bad paint job that used to park at the end of our cul-de-sac? With the bumper sticker that says "What a long strange trip it's been?"

"That's the one. That's Buddy."

"I thought it was abandoned. I kept calling the county to pick it up. But everytime they came, he'd left."

"Yeah, he got annoyed by that. He likes to sleep in the car."

"So he was watching us. And now you have cameras." She waves a hand. "In here. Watching us."

She's not taking this well. She doesn't understand. "I promised Geoffrey I'd look out for you. Couldn't really do that when I was halfway around the world. "

"Geoffrey..." she mutters and shakes her head. "So you spied on us?"

"It wasn't like that."

"You put cameras in my home–"

"To keep you safe, Julia. There's nothing I wouldn't do to keep you safe."

* * *

Julia

I can't believe this. He's standing in my kitchen, telling me he had us under surveillance.

All these years, and he didn't bother to show up. But he installed cameras. I could cross the kitchen and grab the shotgun I keep loaded. It's not silver shot, but it would hurt.

I wouldn't reach the door before he stopped me, but I am tempted.

I raise a shaking hand and point out the door. "Get out."

"Julia, listen–"

"No, no more. I'm done talking. You need to leave right now." My voice rises to a shout.

"Mom?" Geo's voice cracks midword. He's standing on the stairs, barefoot. "What's going on?"

"Geo." I lower my hand and make my voice calm. "Everything's fine."

Channing turns and Geo gives him the stink eye. "What's he doing here?" There's a weird glint to his eyes, and his voice sounds unnatural. Snarly.

"It's okay." I scramble around the table, but Channing puts out a hand, blocking my way.

"Julia, stay back."

I open my mouth to argue, but Geo's eyes flash, and his nostrils flare. His wolf prowls there, under the surface.

"Easy, Junior," Channing says.

"Don't call me that." Geo's voice drops into a deeper register and becomes a low growl.

Goosebumps break out over my body. That sound, coming from my boy... he sounds like a wild animal. A wolf.

"Your mom and I were having an argument," Channing says in a low, calm voice. "She's angry with me, can you smell it? I fu–messed up, and we're dealing with it. But everything's chill." He takes a step forward, putting himself more squarely between Geo and me. "We're gonna have pizza, see?"

Geo tilts his head in a fluid motion. His body hunches

forward, like he's going to fall to all fours. A whine escapes his throat.

"That's right, Geo." I force my voice to be pleasant, but it shakes a little. I need to get my emotions under control.

Geo's hand clutches the banister so hard, something crunches. Is that fur growing along his wrist?

I suck in a breath. "Geo?"

My son's body curls forward and shudders like his spine isn't under his control.

I can't stop the panic rising in me. I start forward but stop myself. I want to go to Geo and help him, but there's nothing I can do.

"Geo," Channing says in a firm voice. "It's gonna be okay. There's a lot of energy running through your body right now. That's your instinct to protect your mom. It brings your wolf to the surface. Your wolf will always come to the surface when there's danger. Or when you're angry. And some day, when you find your mate. But your mom is safe. So quiet the wolf."

"I...I can't," he chokes, but the words come out more as a snarl than a human utterance.

Geo's teeth are growing too big for his mouth.

I gasp, and his gaze jerks to me, pupils narrowing, irises glowing. His jaw falls open, and he snarls. I flinch, my entire body freezing, sensing a predator in the room.

Channing reaches behind him, pressing me back. Then he steps forward, blocking my view of my son with his body.

"Okay, Geo. You're just going to have to shift and run this energy off, then."

Geo snarl-whimpers, a trapped animal sound.

"Geo," Channing orders, his voice deep and echoing, otherworldly. *"Shift."*

Geo's body hits the floor. I can't see what's happening, but the sounds—grunts and growls and claws scrabbling on the floor—are horrible. I shrink behind Channing, my fingers digging into his tight t-shirt. I don't know what else to do but hold on.

"That's it. You've got it." Channing's voice rings out with confidence. "You did it, buddy."

I peek around Channing's biceps.

A huge white wolf stands in front of the stairs. His body is the size of a German Shepherd, but his head is even bigger. He's so huge, but this isn't even full size. In a few years, he'll be bigger than a Timberwolf.

Eldritch green eyes flash, and the wolf drops his head.

There are shreds of the t-shirt and sweatpants littering the floor around him. At least he wasn't wearing shoes.

Channing approaches slowly. I hold my breath as he extends a hand, but Geo's wolf doesn't crouch and pounce or growl and bite. He sniffs the tips of Channing's fingers and pushes his nose against them, then licks them.

"That's right, you know me." Channing turns his head and grins at me, and the dimple catches me by surprise. "He recognizes my scent. He knows we're family."

I press both hands to my face, as if they can hold in all my emotions. Fear, shock, relief, elation.

Channing kneels and runs his hand over the wolf's flanks. "Good job, Junior. Only got a little stuck. Next time will be easier, I promise. It just takes practice." The wolf not only lets Channing pet him, he leans into Channing, rubbing against him and poking his nose everywhere.

Channing chuckles and looks back at me. "He's white, like Geoffrey."

The wolf shoves his head in Channing's face and licks. Channing's deep laugh echoes around the room, filling the empty corners. Righting all the wrongs.

"Come on. Let's go meet your mom."

My heart leaps out of my chest, but when Channing extends a hand, I take it and let him place my palm on the wolf's white back. The fur is thick and strong but softer than I expected. I suck in a sob.

"He's beautiful, isn't he?" Channing says.

"So beautiful."

"See? Nothing to be scared of." Channing keeps narrating in his strong, smooth voice. "Strong emotion can bring on the change, and teenagers have a hard time controlling their emotions. But don't worry, you'll learn to control it."

The wolf whines.

"No, you did good. You did just what you're supposed to do. And I'm with you now. I'm gonna help." Channing rises and heads to the back door. "Now we let your wolf run. That's all he needs. This way."

The wolf follows, its claws clicking on the kitchen tile.

They're out the door. I stand there a moment before I can get my trembling legs to follow.

Channing comes to meet me at the door. "We're going for a run," he tells me in a firm tone that allows no argument. "He needs to get used to his wolf form."

I nod. I was opposed to this, but now that we're in the moment and it's happening, I'm so grateful Channing knows what to do. That he knows what to say and how to guide Geo.

The white wolf is already halfway up the hill, sniffing around a tree. Channing was right. Geo's wolf needs to be in the wild.

Not Geo's wolf. *Geo.* He's my son in wolf form as much as he is as a human.

"If you go to the truck, you'll find a bunch of t-shirts and sweatpants. I bought them cheap." He looks past me to the crop circle of shredded fabric by the stairs and grimaces. "Next time will be easier. Every time, it gets easier."

"That's good." My voice wobbles.

"Hey." Channing puts a hand to my cheek. "You okay?"

"I'm okay." I'm blinking back tears, overwhelmed with all the feelings, but as long as Geo is okay, I'll live.

"Nothing to be worried about. I'm not going to let anything happen to him, Julia. I promise."

Chapter Five

Channing

I stride out to Geo, who's sniffing the base of a pine tree, scenting all the animal visitors to his territory. He looks back at me, his tongue lolling out.

"Go ahead." I wave a hand to give permission. "It's your home, and I know you want to."

The wolf wastes no time cocking a leg and marking the tree.

"That's it."

The wolf finishes and trots to the next pine.

I breathe in the night, and the tightness in my chest eases. My nose is still singed with Julia's panic. She did her best, but she was afraid for her son.

Even so, Geo's shift went better than I thought it would. For a few awful seconds, I was sure Julia would slip past me, and Geo would pounce. It didn't help that all our emotions were high. Part of me wants to go back and comfort Julia, but the best thing I can do to help her is to guide Geo. She'll be okay.

When I turn, Geo is waiting nearby, looking up expectantly.

"I'm coming," I say. "We're going to go on a good long run. And don't worry, when the time comes, I'll give the order, and your wolf will let you shift back, no problem."

Getting stuck is the biggest fear. It's hard to let your wolf come, take over your body. A part of you fears you'll never get it back. New wolves sometimes have a hard time changing back.

Every alpha takes the time to guide the young wolves in his pack. When it's time, he can use his alpha voice to command the wolf to shift, if necessary.

I'm not an alpha. I've never led a pack. But when Geo was struggling, I gave the command. Somehow I used the alpha voice. I didn't know I could do that.

I strip off my shirt, which is too tight anyway, and kick off my boots and jeans. The question of boxers or briefs is easy when you're a werewolf. The less clothes you wear, the better. When we're on a mission we wear the boxers made from a material flexible enough to stay on when we shift, so we're not caught with our dongs hanging in the wind when we shift back. It was developed by the military when we were on the shifter ops team. I guess our government thought having naked soldiers in the field would be unseemly.

I take a deep breath and call my wolf. The Change envelops me. The world contorts, shimmering as if everything around me is changing instead of my own perspective. Tingles fizz up my spine.

Alpha's Command

Shifting isn't supposed to hurt. Sometimes I get a brief flash of feeling, like I've hit my funny bone the wrong way. If I'm on a mission and taken a bullet, that's another story, but shifting can help heal wounds faster. Or slower, depending on the severity of the wound.

My early shifts were painful because I was fighting it. My brother talked me through them until I learned to relax. Shifting should be as easy as a sneeze. Human one minute, wolf the next.

I'll tell Geo this once we're both in human form, but now it's time to run.

Geo's holding back, giving me space to shake out the tingles from the Change. I push forward and rub my body along his. He staggers a little and then presses back. Wolves are affectionate, and we need touch. Geo needs to get used to the feel of being in his fur.

Once we're done greeting each other, I point my nose up the hill and break into a run. He follows me, loping up the incline.

Behind us, the house glows with the light in the kitchen window. There's a dark figure there, watching. Julia.

A squirrel darts in front of us, flashing its tail and disappearing over the hill. I sense Geo straining to run after it, but he doesn't. He waits, following my lead. I bark to give him permission, and with a yip, he dashes off, giving chase.

I trot after him. We'll run a few miles and chase as many squirrels as he wants. I'll show him the boundaries of his territory, where his father marked the trees long ago. We'll mark them afresh and find the biggest hill overlooking Geo's land. I'll teach him to howl.

The house behind us has disappeared. I unleash my limbs and race after Geo, giving into the speed and strength and beauty of being a wolf.

When we get to the top of the ridge, I give a bark and Geo stops, turning to wait for my command. I shift into human form.

"Now you," I instruct.

Geo crouches, lowering his snout as if concentrating, but nothing happens. I wait. I need to give him time to figure this out on his own. He whines a little.

"Shift back," I tell him. "Just remember the feeling of being in your human form and move your consciousness there."

He whines a little more. The air around him shimmers as the Change starts to come on, but then it stops again.

"You can do it. I'll help you if you need me to, but I want you to practice on your own. You just move your consciousness to your human form. Imagine you're in your human form now."

More shimmering, but still no shift.

"It's okay. It takes a while to get the hang of it." I try to remember how I learned. What helped me. "It's like...you bookmark in your mind the energy signature of each shape. So right now, bookmark how it feels to be a wolf. *Now shift.*" I use alpha command on him again.

The Change takes over, and he's in his young man form, crouched on the ground. "That's it. Good job."

He straightens and looks at me uncertainly. He's not used to being naked in front of others the way those of us who grew up in a pack are.

"Now bookmark in your mind how it feels in this body."

I have no idea if he understands what I'm saying. It's a hard thing to put words to. It's just a sensation.

"Do you remember what it felt like to be in your wolf form?"

Geo gives a single, solemn nod.

I smile. "Good. Now shift back." I don't use the alpha command. I let him seek it on his own.

He tenses, softening his knees like a martial arts fighter. His eyes close, and intense concentration screws up the features of his face. A wolf-growl rockets from his throat, but it seems to surprise him, and he pulls back, eyes flying open and seeking mine.

I smile. "That was right, Geo. Try again."

He shakes his head and shrugs his shoulders like a boxer about to get in the ring.

"Remember what it was like to be in wolf form and just put your entire consciousness there. You have to leave this consciousness. Leave the human thoughts. Find the wolf instincts."

The air around Geo shimmers. I hear the crack of joints, a whimper, then a snarl, and then he's a wolf again.

I reward him by dropping back into my wolf and racing ahead, challenging him to keep up.

* * *

Julia

After what feels like hours, something moves in the trees.

I gave up pacing and waiting, and started cleaning. I

wiped down the fridge, the oven, and the microwave. Reorganized the cans in the pantry. The kitchen has never been so clean.

I'm scrubbing out the coffee pot when a flash of movement ripples down the hill.

After they left, I stood at the kitchen sink, staring past the patio. Flashes of white move between the pines. It was easy to tell the two wolves apart—one is big, but the other is a monster. Channing's wolf could almost stand shoulder to shoulder with me. Not an animal you'd want to meet on a hike.

I knew Geo might turn into a wolf although it's not certain with a half-breed. I tried to imagine it, rehearsing different scenarios. I'm a control freak. I like to plan. But the way Geo's body contorted, like he was in pain...the way that growl erupted from my baby boy's mouth—I froze. All the advice from the teen psychology books flew out of my head.

Channing knew what to do. When he gave that command in that weird echoey voice, Geo obeyed.

I'm in a whole new world, and none of my rules apply. I need to get it together.

I stood there for a while after they left, my arms wrapped around myself, and let the aftermath of all my adrenaline shudder through me.

Then, I followed orders. I went to the truck and got the clothes. There were four bags of them stuffed behind the front seats. Channing must have bought out the store. I left one bag in the truck because Channing might need it. Now his weird outfit when he showed up this morning makes sense. He must have shifted earlier and not had a proper change of clothes.

And I judged him for it. I decided he was being his usual irresponsible self and assumed the worst. And he let me.

I set a pair of clothes on the picnic table, like I used to do for Geoffrey. Geoffrey would joke that he didn't mind walking around naked. Some nights, when Geo was asleep and Channing was out, he would ignore the pile of clothes and come find me.

I haven't thought about that in years. Life rolls on even when you're stuck in your grief. It's a blessing and a curse. The memories of my late husband don't have the sting they used to. I can remember the good times, the laughter, without the searing pain. It's bittersweet.

If you're reading this, something happened to me. I hoped this day would never come, but it has.

I read the letter Geoffrey left late at night. After I'd put Geo, only three and still confused about why his father couldn't come tuck him in, to bed.

Channing will be there for you.

By then, Channing was long gone.

And now he's back, and he's like a different person.

He's more like Geoffrey. That thought brings on a streak of longing so deep it rocks me. Longing to let Channing in. Let him stay. Let him take Geoffrey's place. But no. Channing isn't Geoffrey. And he's not here for me. He's here for Geo.

For me to imagine anything...*romantic*... happening with him is foolish. It's wrong. I should feel big sisterly toward him. Even if he weren't Geoffrey's brother, he would be far too young for me. Besides, he's in some kind of high-risk security work. Very dangerous. I've had enough dangerous for a lifetime.

I'm not going to fall in love with a soldier again. That ended far too painfully for me.

I grab my glass of wine, the one Channing poured for me, and take a healthy swallow. I couldn't sit and eat while they were gone, my stomach flipping over. But now they're finally back.

The two wolves emerge from the trees, loping towards the house. They stop before the patio, just outside the circle of flood lights. Their brown markings make them blend into the background, but if I squint hard, I can see them. The smaller one raises his head, rubbing his cheek against the larger one. It is so sweet it nearly brings me to my knees.

It also somewhat offends me that Channing should be able to win Geo's trust and affection in a few short hours after abandoning him all this time. But that doesn't change the gratitude I have for Channing right now.

That he *did* show up. That he's here for Geo when Geo needs him most.

I resist the urge to run out there, interrupt the moment. Their movements are graceful and awe-inspiring.

The larger one–Channing–waits and paces back a few steps, facing the smaller wolf. Like a teacher with a pupil. Now that they're standing still, I can pick out the subtle differences in their markings.

The big wolf raises his head–and rises to hind legs, somehow morphing back into human form. Fur disappears, his head and jaw reshapes. It happens in an instant, but slow enough I can pick out the exact moment the wolf becomes man, becomes Channing.

A very big, very naked Channing. He's standing outside the circle of light, but there's no mistaking the solid, grooved lines of his muscles. The tapered obliques under his bulging arms, the giant, powerful thighs.

He turns to face the house, and steps into the light. Nestled in the crisp blond hair is his alarmingly large dick. My core cramps, hard. I shouldn't think of him this way. Shoudn't be attracted to my dead husband's younger brother. I should think...brotherly thoughts about him.

Something shatters in front of me. The wine glass slipped out of my nerveless fingers and smashed into the sink.

"Shoot." I reach into the sink and slice my finger.

The kitchen door flies open.

"Everything all right?" Channing stands in the doorway, completely naked. The warm light gilds the strong breadth of his shoulders and casts the ridges and contours of his chest in relief.

"Yes," I blurt, grabbing a nearby dish towel. "I dropped my wine glass."

He looks at me with concern. His bare skin glows with the barest hint of sweat. His thighs are huge and powerful. His Adonis belt cuts a V leading right to his...

I force my eyes to Channing's face. "Did it go okay?" My voice is breathless.

"Yeah." He relaxes. "It went great." He doesn't care that he's buck naked, giant dick swinging in the breeze. Shifters don't care about nudity the way humans do.

I hold the dishcloth up, creating a screen between his gorgeous god-like body and my greedy gaze. "I left your clothes on the picnic table. Do you mind?"

"Oh, yeah, sure." He pivots, mooning me.

And what a beautiful full moon it is. The slick muscles of his back lead to two defined dimples above the smooth swell of his ass.

A strangled noise escapes my throat.

Channing halts and looks back. "You sure you're okay?"

I wave the dishcloth at him, unable to speak. He ducks out of the house, and I stare at the mess I made. My chest is flushed, my skin uncomfortably hot.

My son bursts through the door, bringing with him a welcome wave of cool air.

"Mom!" He's breathless. "I shifted." Geo's bright-eyed and flushed from his run. The scent of pine and the night clings to his hair. He's wearing the nondescript t-shirt and sweatpants I set out for him. The t-shirt fits, but the sweatpants are way too loose.

"I saw, I saw," I say.

"It was epic." Geo strides into the room, looking more like a man and so much less like the little boy I raised. How did this happen? "I'm so strong as a wolf. And really fast. We went far–way up to the top of the ridge and around the back side. Uncle Channing took me all the way up to the lookout. And I practiced shifting. I learned how to bookmark my different shapes."

"That's great, *mijo*." Relief hits me so hard, I tear up.

Behind Geo, Channing enters the house. He's wearing

the same too-small shirt stretched tight over his broad chest and his jeans. He's gorgeous.

"We're going again tomorrow night," Geo says. "And Uncle Channing says we can go for an even longer time this weekend."

"He did, did he?" I narrow my eyes at Channing, but I'm not upset they're planning more outings. Channing gives me that lazy, lopsided grin of his. The dimples wink.

Eggs aren't dropping from my ovaries. They're not.

"Can we, Mom? We were careful. Uncle Channing's going to teach me how to shift safely and be responsible."

"Of course." I reach up to touch Geo's hair. I used to ruffle his silky black hair all the time, but not since he shot up taller than me. But for the moment, the cynical teen's fallen away, replaced by an enthusiastic kid.

"Uncle Channing knows best."

"She finally admits it." Channing winks.

"Thanks." Geo leans in, hugging me hard enough to squeeze the air from my lungs. He lifts me off my feet, and I wheeze.

"Easy, Junior," Channing admonishes. "You're stronger than you think."

"Oh sorry." Geo sets me back down. "Can I have pizza now? Uncle Channing wouldn't let me kill the squirrel. I'm starving."

"Go ahead," I say, and Geo dives for the table. Should I make him wash his hands first?

Too late, he's flipped open a pizza box and stuffed three slices into his mouth at once.

I turn away before I start nagging him to chew.

"Thank you," I say to Channing. Meaning it. "For everything."

He accepts my thanks with a dip of his head and moves close, into my space. "Have you eaten yet?"

I shake my head.

His nostrils flare, and he takes the dish rag and catches my hand. "You got yourself good."

"I was distracted."

His head dips to mine, and a wave of his spicy, wild scent washes over me. I don't mean to, but I find myself leaning into him, wanting more.

He raises his head, his green eyes catching mine. My breath stalls in my throat. My heart thumps. A swell of heat rolls over me. *I'm not attracted to Geoffrey's baby brother. I'm not. I feel only brotherly thoughts about him.*

"Sit." He nudges me to the table. "I'll get something to clean this."

"The first aid kit is—"

"On the top shelf in the bathroom. I remember." His dimples flash, and he disappears.

I sag into a chair. My cheeks warm. Another hot flash? Or was it the wine?

That must be it. The wine's affecting me. I haven't finished the glass, but I drank on an empty stomach. That's why my insides are fluttery.

No other reason.

Geo's eaten a whole pizza already and is sucking on some hot wings. I remember Geoffrey eating like this when he returned from a long run. Shifting forms burns a lot of calories.

I push a second pizza box towards him. "Eat up, *mijo*." He gives me a grateful look and stuffs a stack of three pizza slices into his mouth.

Channing returns and kneels in front of me. He's so big, the kitchen shrinks around him, but his hands on mine are gentle. He checks my finger for shreds of glass. Once he's satisfied, he bandages it with deft movements. With every touch, tingles run up my arms.

I find my voice. "You've done this before."

"A time or two."

"Shifters don't need bandages." Their healing powers can take care of anything short of decapitation. *Or a blast from an IED.*

He looks solemn, as if he can follow the line of my thoughts. "We do when we're trying to pass." Pass as humans, he means. "And I've fought alongside humans at times."

I drop my eyes to the bandage. "Thanks."

"Anytime," he murmurs, taking my hand and turning it over. Tingles race over my skin where he touches me.

I dip my head and gulp in the air. Channing moves away, out of my space, but I feel his presence pressing on me, a delicious weight. I've never been so aware of anyone in my life.

After he cleans up the glass, a chair scrapes across the kitchen tile, Channing taking his seat.

"Careful, Uncle Channing," Geo says. "That table leg is loose."

"Ah. I remember your dad fixing it the day he bought it. Let's fix it tomorrow. I'll wait until after school, so you can help."

"Really?"

"Yeah."

I grab a slice of pizza and nibble, keeping my eyes on my plate and trying to get my heartbeat under control.

"Do you run as a wolf every night?" Geo asks.

Channing shakes his head. "No. Not every night. Every full moon, for sure. And if I need to let off steam. You'll probably need to run quite a bit as a teenager. Hormones are raging through you, way more intense than a human experiences. You'll get attracted to girls at school, and it will nearly make you shift in your seat."

"Channing!" I can't stop the shocked sound of my voice. I really don't want him giving Geo sex advice. I remember what a man-whore he was when he lived here.

"What?" He tosses that lazy grin my way again. "It's true. Better I warn him now than have him actually lose control in front of humans." He turns his gaze on Geo. "You understand that you can never, ever speak of this with any human? Not with your best friend. Not with your girlfriend, if you date a human. Not with anyone. You can't shift in a fight with boys at school. You can't use your superhuman strength to play sports. You have to hide what you are. That's the most important thing I have to teach you."

"Why? Because I would scare humans?"

"Yes. But..." Channing's gaze shifts toward me, and I can tell he doesn't want me to hear what's coming next. "There are humans who do know we exist, and..." –another concerned glance my way–"and some of those who know like to hunt our kind."

I'm sure the color drains from my face because I go ice cold.

Channing reaches over and covers my hand. "Nothing's ever going to happen to Geo. I promise. My ops team is the best in the world. If any danger ever came this way, I would know it and prevent it from touching Geo."

I suck in a breath. So that's why he installed the security at the house. It makes sense. But what doesn't make sense is why he did it in secret. Why he waited until we were at Disneyland and came while we were gone. Why he was watching us all along but never stopped in. Never made contact.

I don't understand it.

I'm realizing there's so much more to Channing than I thought, but I'm not sure what it is. I'd written him off as an irresponsible, reckless, self-involved kid. Or sometimes, when I gave him more credit, I thought maybe it was too painful for him to be around me and Geo. That he didn't want to face his grief over losing his brother.

Maybe that was it, but it still doesn't quite fit. Because if he was protecting us all along, wouldn't that mean he was facing his brother's death?

Channing and Geo continue their chat, reliving their run. After inhaling enough pizza to send them into a food coma, they rise and clear the table. They stand at the kitchen sink, cleaning it out and doing the dishes. One short, one tall. One dark haired, one blond. Like Geoffrey and Channing used to do.

The memory tugs me, but instead of the pain of loss, there's a nostalgic ache and a sense of satisfaction. The scene looks normal, looks right. Channing fits right into the space his brother left.

This is a moment I had envisioned initially, after Geoffrey died. That Channing would be around, playing uncle. Another adult to lean on. A shifter. A connection to Geoffrey. But Channing never came back.

I reach for my old hardened resentment, but it slips away. I'm not going to ruin this peaceful moment. Geo needs it.

"All right, Junior." Channing claps Geo on the shoulder. "Time to turn in. School starts early, and you need your rest if we're going to run tomorrow night."

Without protest, without dragging his feet, Geo nods and turns to obey.

"Night, Mom." He leans down and catches me in a hug.

"Good night, baby."

"I'm sorry for... you know." There's a little catch in his voice, and I know he's reliving the tense moments before he shifted.

I squeeze him hard. "It's okay. You did nothing wrong. It just took me by surprise."

Geo leans back, tossing his hair out of his eyes, so he can peer at me. He looks unsure. "It'll be better next time." There's a question in his voice, one I can't answer.

Behind him, Channing is nodding. "It will," he confirms, and Geo's body relaxes.

"I love you," I tell my son, and he mumbles, "Love you," back before releasing me and disappearing up the stairs.

Leaving me with Channing. Alone.

The air thickens between us, turning solid. His eyes glow a little in the low light.

I could close my eyes, but he'll be there, waiting for me in my mind. Over six feet of hard, golden body. The image of him naked burned itself into my brain. I saw my brother-in-law naked, and worse, I didn't want to look away.

I don't want to look away now. The world has narrowed to his sharp green gaze.

"Relax, Jewels. He's going to be fine. I promise." He's doing that thing again, using that smooth, commanding voice.

I bob my head, drawing in a deep breath.

The way his gaze caresses my face isn't brotherly. It's intimate. Affectionate.

"What you did with Geo—"

He puts a finger to his lips and points up the stairs. Right. Shifter hearing.

He takes my hand, pulling me out of the chair. My pulse leaps, but I let him lead me out to the patio.

"We can talk here." He turns. His hand envelops mine. His skin is warm to the touch. Shifters run a little hotter than a normal human if I remember correctly.

I shiver for no reason.

Channing frowns. "Cold?"

"No, this is good." I'm still overheated. I pull my hand from Channing's and sink into an Adirondack chair. Channing stays standing, frowning down at me.

"What is it?" I ask, unused to a frown on his face.

"I need to sand these chairs," he mutters and shakes his head to dismiss the thought. He snaps into a mode I've never seen before, intent and serious. "Tonight turned out all right," he says like he's making a report to his commanding officer. Is this what he's like on missions? My pulse picks up speed. I love this side of him.

"Geo did well, followed my lead. There was a moment of panic at the end that he might not be able to change back, but I talked him through it."

"Thank you." I can't say it enough.

"No problem." He sinks to his haunches. I'm sitting, and he's crouching, and he's still my height, able to look into my eyes. "I'm sorry I wasn't here for his first time, but I'm here now. And I'll stay as long as he needs me," he tells me.

"Thanks. I'm glad. You know, for Geo."

"For Geo." His voice deepens.

His gaze drops to my lips. Time slows, stops. My lips tingle, and I lick them. When did the world start spinning slower?

"Julia..." He's so close his breath caresses my face.

I squeeze my legs together as if I could squeeze away the throbbing pressure building in my core.

It's a chilly September night, and I'm burning up.

It's not the wine. It's not the heat or hot flashes. It's my libido, roaring to life.

I didn't think I had a sex drive anymore. Sure, I have a vibrator and give myself an orgasm once or twice a week, like clockwork. But perving on a sexy guy? It's been years since I've done that. And this one is far too young for me.

I've got to get a grip. This is not the time for my dry and dusty vagina to wake up. One of us has to be an adult here.

I lean back, and the spell is broken.

"For Geo," I repeat, and something in his face shutters. He looks older, harder, somehow.

He stands. "I'll get my kit. I'll sleep on the floor."

"You can have the couch," I say.

"Naw, it's too small. I won't fit."

"You're not that big," I say.

His cheek curves. "I assure you I am."

Oh. My. God.

Why did that make my nipples hard? I rise. "Let me know if you need anything." His brows rise, and my eyes widen. "A pillow, I mean. A toothbrush."

"I get it," he says. His voice is back to neutral.

I have a crazy urge to put out my hand to shake his. Put some distance between us. Instead, I say goodnight and walk away on weak legs, willing my heart to beat normally.

* * *

Channing

I wait until Julia's safe inside her room for the night. Then I make the rounds, locking the house, checking the bolts and alarm system, securing the place. I usually activate the security system remotely, after the cameras tell me Geo and Julia have settled in for the night. I've never done it in person before.

I roll out my sleeping bag on her office floor. Not sure why I want to torture myself, but I need to be enveloped in her scent. My cock is so hard it hurts, but I welcome the pain. It's a fitting punishment.

Tonight, when we spoke on the patio, I almost kissed her. Less than twenty-four hours, and I'm already fucking up.

I'd hoped her anger and low opinion of me would build a

moat between us. I crave her forgiveness, but I don't deserve it. I figured her disgust and distrust would help me keep my distance. My brother's scent on her, that ring on her finger should help me keep my distance.

Yet she looked at me tonight, and instead of anger or hurt, I saw something else.

Attraction.

Desire.

She's feeling it, too.

But I can't mention it. What sort of asshole would I be to point it out? "By the way, I can smell your arousal."

I can't do this to Julia. To my brother. But knowing me, it's only a matter of time before I fuck up again.

I'll keep to the mission. Teach Geo how to be a wolf and how to be a man. It won't make up for the years I missed, but it'll help.

Once Geo's set, I'll disappear. Again. It'll hurt, but they've gone through it before.

I'll do what I came to do and get out of here before I fuck up their family any more than I already have.

Chapter Six

Julia

There's an ache between my legs. I twist, trapped in the sheets.

A deep voice murmurs. "Julia."

Channing.

I roll towards him. He's shirtless in the moonlight because, of course, he is. Is he naked? I can't tell.

I stretch my arms above my head, letting my hair cascade over the pillow. I'm in a sexy nightie, low cut with lace draped over my cleavage. "I've been waiting for you."

His eyes are green flares in the dark. He puts a hand on my leg and slides it upward in a slow, inexorable ascent.

I lick my lips and let my legs fall open.

"Julia." He rips the sheets away from me and covers me with his hard body.

I raise my head to meet his. His lips find mine. They're firm, yet gentle. A growl rises in his throat. He takes a handful of my hair, controlling the kiss. Heat blooms in my core, and I gasp.

He drags me into his arms, seating me into his lap. His hands grip my ass, pulling me against him. I cant my hips forward, rubbing myself up and down. He is naked, and I'm so wet. Any second now, he's going to slide inside—

A bird shrieks outside my window, and I jerk awake. My core is slick, and my breasts are swollen, heavy.

There's no darkness, no Channing. I'm alone. It was a dream, but it felt so real.

I blink at the sunlight flooding my bedroom. It's way brighter than it should be at six am.

I snap up into a sitting position. What time is it?

The alarm clock reads nine thirteen am. I slept through my alarm.

The hall floor creaks, and my bedroom door glides open.

"Oh, hey, you're awake." Channing leans against the frame, balancing a laundry basket on his opposite hip. "Do you have any laundry? I'm doing a load. Geo showed me your system."

Laundry? System? "What?"

A dimple pops in Channing's cheek. "Never mind. Hang tight, I'll be right back."

He disappears. I rub the sleep out of my eyes and touch my head in horror. My hair is a wild, static-y mess. I'm wearing the low-cut nightie I wore in my dream. My nipples are taut peaks. I grab my comforter and pull it up to my neck.

Channing's footsteps announce his return. He must have walked on the creaky spots of my hardwood floors on purpose. When he wants, he can glide like a cat–though I'd never compare him to a cat unless I wanted to annoy him.

He sails into my bedroom, way too chipper for early morning. "Here you go." He hands me a mug, and the delicious coffee scent wafts over my face.

"Thanks," I mumble. "I overslept. My alarm clock–"

"I turned it off," Channing straightens my bed blankets with one hand and holds a slice of cold pizza with another.

"You did what?"

"You needed sleep." He takes a bite of pizza.

"I can't believe you." I slide out of bed. "I'm late for work."

"You set your own schedule, right?"

"I can't... You can't... I just..."

"Take it easy," Channing soothes. "I gave Geo a ride to school. Don't worry we didn't take my bike. He wasn't feeling the bus this morning, so I took him in the truck. I'm surprised the engine didn't wake you. You really needed sleep, huh?"

I'm an articulate person. I can speak rationally, lay out an argument. But when I open my mouth, I've got nothing.

"Drink your coffee," Channing prompts with his pizza hand, and I automatically stick my nose in the mug. The scent helps to wake me up.

"Good girl." The right side of his mouth quirks up. And that dimple.

Oh my God. I can't believe he called me *good girl*. Worse, I can't believe my reaction to the words.

He saunters to my closet and picks up my laundry basket. He's humming a song–sounds like one of Taylor Swift's new hits.

He catches me staring and salutes me with the slice of pizza. "Pizza for breakfast, I'm telling you." He walks out before I can decide how to kill him.

I make it to my desk in time for my first meeting with Mr. van den Berg. With only a few minutes to get dressed and tame my hair, I didn't have time to hunt Channing down and kill him. But I plan to. Thank God, I automated my follow-ups for the meeting last night before I let him in the house and lost all self control.

Is he going to infiltrate every inch of my house? My life? It's bad enough that I had a sex dream about him. Every time I close my eyes, I relive seeing him naked.

And since when does he do laundry?

My office smells like him. Did he come in here?

I face my computer and try to look professional for the camera.

"Julia," Mr. van den Berg greets me. "I accepted all the changes. The contract should be in your inbox."

"Thank you, sir." I say. A loud banging noise drowns out my words. Someone's hammering something on my roof. I hold up a finger. "Excuse me, one moment."

I mute myself and walk to the window, out of sight of the camera. I wrestle with the ancient sash until it opens—Geoffrey and I were going to replace the windows, and I never got around to it—and holler, "Be quiet! I'm in a meeting!"

The hammering stops.

I smooth my hair and paste a calm smile to my face. When I sit back down at my desk, my boss looks concerned.

"I apologize for the noise," I say. "It won't happen again."

"Not a problem," he says. "Do you have roofers there?"

"Yes, sort of. It's my brother-in-law. He's doing some work around the house, and I didn't realize he'd be fixing the shingles today." On-screen, my reflection's eye twitches. I suck in a deep breath. Calm, rational, in control–that's me.

"Your brother-in-law is still there?"

"Yes, he's going to be staying with us for a while. It's a long story." I hope I don't have to recount it, but Mr. van den Berg looks curious.

"I didn't realize you were so close."

"We haven't seen him for almost ten years," I confess. "Not since Geoffrey's funeral." Normally I wouldn't share so much with a work colleague, but this is my boss, and he's been so supportive.

"I see," my boss says after a pause. "Forgive me if I overstep, but are you comfortable with this situation? Is his presence..." he hesitates as if choosing his words carefully. "Welcome?"

"Oh, yes, of course," I rush to say, touched by his concern. "It was a surprise, but we're glad he's here."

"That's good. Let me know if you need help with anything, Julia. My door is always open."

"Thank you, sir."

I can sense he wants to say more, but he changes the subject to the next steps with the contracts, and I'm all too grateful to focus on work.

As soon as the meeting's done, I'm going to kill Channing and bury him beyond the patio, a slice of cold pizza in his mouth.

A few seconds after I log off with Mr. van den Berg,

something clatters on the roof. Channing swings into the open window.

He's half-dressed in jeans and boots. No shirt. His chest glistens with a light sheen of sweat.

"Miss me?" He shows me his dimples.

I rise out of my chair, pointing at his bare chest. "I'm going to kill you."

He cocks his head into the *aw shucks* position. "What did I do?"

I tick the items off my fingers. "Turned off my alarm clock. Made me late. Started hammering things in the middle of my meeting with my boss."

"Yeah, my bad. I can wait until later to finish the shingles. Get Geo to help."

"Channing Eugene Armstrong, you will not take my son onto the roof—"

He cocks his head. "You do know he's virtually indestructible, don't you? Shifters heal—" Steam must have come from my ears because Channing waves his hands. "Fine, no roof. Who was that you were talking to?"

"What?" The subject change has me reeling.

"The old guy who sounds like he has a stick up his ass."

"He does not sound like that," I sputter. "Mr. van den Berg is my boss, and he's good to us."

Channing's eyes narrow. "How so?"

"He pays me an excellent salary with a generous benefits package. And he's helping get Geo into a new school."

"And what does he ask you to do in return?" His voice is silky and deep, dangerous.

"Nothing but my job," I say. "You've got the wrong idea. Our interactions are completely appropriate. Professional."

"Except that he's taken an interest in you and Geo's personal life." His jaw clenches.

"He's been nothing but kind. I know you have no idea how hard it is to raise a kid by yourself, but let me assure you, I needed the help."

Channing flinches, and I feel guilty for bringing out the big guns.

"I know," he says softly. He's moved close into my space, and the fresh wave of his outdoorsy scent makes me dizzy.

I hold up a hand to ward him off. "Not just wads of drug dealer money. I'm a lawyer. I make a decent wage. I needed a different kind of support."

The dimple's back. "For the record, I've never worked for a drug dealer. I've shot quite a few, though."

"Enough," I say.

Channing gives me a sly smile and a wave of heat washes over me. My palm hovers over his bare chest. I snatch it back and cross my arms to remove the temptation of touching him. It's shameful how much I want to. "Where is your shirt?"

He shrugs. "I got hot on the roof. Speaking of which, when is your next meeting? I want to nail down these shingles before dusk."

I want to tell him to eff off, but I guess I do need the shingles replaced. "Wait until my lunch break. I have to go to the grocery store then."

"Groceries are covered. Tell me what you want to get. Geo and I already put in an order–I'm having it delivered."

I open my mouth. Close it. If I don't calm down, my head is going to explode.

I just asserted that I needed more help, right? So I can't really tell him I don't want him helping. Laundry and groceries were at the top of my to-do list today.

It's infuriating how helpful he's being. I can't even kill him. How would I plead my case in court? He cleaned my house and ordered dinner, so I shot him?

Shooting him won't work, anyway. I don't have any silver bullets.

Instead of strangling him, I stand inches away from Channing's bare chest, glaring like a freak. It'd be so easy for him to close the distance between us, his arms would hitch me up against him, and I'd wrap my legs around him and rub against his hard body, like in my dream...

Channing stoops, so he's right in my face. "Relax, Julia." His lips hover right over mine. One inch, and they'd be touching.

"Get out," I growl, and he chuckles, backing away until he's sitting on the windowsill, then lets himself tip backward, out of sight.

I rush to the window, expecting to see him sprawled and moaning on the lawn, but he's fine, hanging from one hand off my gutter. Until it cracks under his weight and he falls, taking the gutters with him. "Sorry," he calls. "I'll fix it!"

I slam the window shut, grinding my teeth so hard Channing can probably hear it on the front lawn.

* * *

I'm still seething when I head to the kitchen for lunch. Channing wasn't kidding about the grocery delivery. A little after noon a car pulled up, and a gangly kid, identical to the one who delivered the pizza, carried armfuls of brown bags to the house. I half expect to come down to a table full of grocery bags filled with melting ice cream, but Channing put most of it away.

Geo had a heavy hand in choosing what to order. The freezer is full of frozen waffle fries and pizza rolls, and there are twelve gigantic boxes of sugary cereal, the kind I never buy unless we're camping. I add this to the list of Channing's sins, but when I open the fridge, a brilliant forest of green and red lettuce greets me. There's even fresh basil. Beside the coffee pot is a fancy cheese platter, the type I'd buy to take to a party, along with boxes of three different types of crackers. And a jar of my favorite green olives. When I was pregnant, I ate a jar of Castelvetrano olives a day. I craved them, and Geoffrey drove all over town finding the fancy wine shops that sold them.

Channing must have remembered the story. Geo was a baby when Channing moved in with us. He was a wild teen, slipping in and out of the house at odd hours. I never would've thought he'd noticed or cared.

I'm beginning to realize I don't know Channing at all.

* * *

Channing

The sun's high, and it's hot on the roof. I'd put on a shirt out of respect for Julia, but within six seconds it'd be soaked with sweat. I called my friend Buddy, my shifter friend in the area, and he has time to help me with these construction projects. He can get me a deal on new windows, too.

I should run all this by Julia. She's stressed this morning and annoyed by my presence. It's easier to tell her after the fact than ask permission. More fun, too. She's so cute when she's mad.

My phone buzzes, and I pull it out. The screen reads Deke, so I answer with a grin. "Miss me, Daddy?"

"No."

I wait, but he says nothing, so I prompt, "What's up?"

"I just dropped the triplets off at Bad Bear mountain."

"Just now?" I do a quick calculation. "It's been thirty-six hours."

"I know. Long story." Deke's voice promises a world of hurt to anyone who probes further, so I don't. "I did some digging. Turns out the Terrible Threes heard about the fight club on a new app. There's a secret chat room that's frequented by shifters, most of them teenagers."

"Okay."

"I made them show me the app and read the messages. This guy Hannibal? He's on there. And he challenged several shifter teens to meet him there to fight. The triplets took the bait."

A chill washes over me. "He lured them there."

"Exactly. He's up to something. I can't prove it, but that's what my instincts say."

"I knew it. I couldn't smell his animal."

"I have Kylie hacking the app and digging around to see

what she can find. I'd ask you to help, but I know you're on a mission."

"Yeah." I look down at the shingle in my hand. "It's more complex than I thought it would be. But ping me if you need to."

"Will do. Keep your eyes and ears peeled." He hangs up.

I rub at the knots in my chest. An app for shifter teens? It makes sense. Puberty sucks. It would help to have a pack of friends who understand how hard it is, especially for shifters like Geo who live apart from his kind.

But it's dangerous. Apps can be hacked, or someone like Hannibal can show up and prey on the unsuspecting teens. Technology changes everything.

A growl rumbles through me. My wolf wants to hunt. I don't know what sort of animal that freak Hannibal was, but I want to take a bite out of him. Especially if I find him hanging around Flagstaff. Our meeting with him was too close to Julia's place for comfort.

Julia's tense voice drifts up to me. She's in the kitchen, talking to someone on the phone. The woman has two phones—one for work, one for personal, and she's on the work one most of the day.

I pocket my cell and swing down from the roof. Her back is to me, and her shoulders have risen halfway to her ears.

"I understand it's the beginning of the year," Julia says in a calm-but-frustrated tone. "I'm asking you to give me his transcript so far. No, I don't want to wait until December. No, I– Yes, I can hold." She blows out a breath and growls to herself.

She's eaten some slices of cheese and half the bottle of

olives, my wolf notes with satisfaction. He wants to feed her up.

I swing open the door and deliberately scuff my feet on the mat, so she'll hear me.

She glances up at me and holds up a hand. The person on the other end of the line squawks, and Julia rubs her forehead. "Yes, the last available transcript—"

I hear the sharp tones of some irritated administrator on the other end giving her hassle. "I don't have any Sanchez in the system."

"My last name is Sanchez. His last name is Armstrong. A-R-M-S-T-R-O-N-G."

Julia's work phone starts ringing. She pulls it out of her back pocket and glares at the screen.

"Let me." I hold out my hand for the phone with the school administrator.

She backs away with a little shake of her head, clutching both phones in her hand.

I hate that she's stressed. That she has the weight of the world on her shoulders with no one to give her a break. I hate that it's my fault. My wolf wants to pull her into the circle of my arms and comfort her. But she'd never allow that.

I advance with shifter speed and pluck the phone right from her hand.

* * *

Julia

One second, I'm getting the runaround from a school

administrator with a voice like a Brillo pad. The next, I'm talking to air.

I answer the call from Kim, the opposing counsel on an acquisition my boss is attempting, while half-listening to Channing.

"Hello, there, who am I speaking to?" Channing holds the phone to his ear. He winks at me, flashing that dimpled grin that probably gets him into every woman's pants. "Hi, Barbara. How are you?" Channing purrs, his voice silky smooth. "I know you're busy today, but let me say, you have a beautiful voice."

I roll my eyes but turn away, confident he can handle Barbara. "Mr. van den Berg is not willing to budge on any of those items. There may be wiggle room on the severance packages, but that's it," I tell Kim. "I will take a look at your mark-ups, but I can already tell you, it's non-negotiable."

I hear Channing charming Barbara into sending the transcript without delay. "I appreciate that, Barbara. Send it to..." he glances at me, and I point to Woodman Prep's address listed on the forms I set on the counter.

He's using that *aw shucks* tilt of his head. It works, even over the phone. Damn.

Kim tells me she will go back to her boss again.

"Great. If you think it would help to schedule a sit-down with the major players and hammer this out in person, van den Berg and I can probably come out to New York next week." I can't believe I'm offering to travel for this. I hate traveling because of all the pre-arranging it takes to make sure Geo's covered, but some negotiations just don't happen between lawyers. You have to get the players in the room together.

I end the call with Kim at the same time Channing ends the call with Brillo Barbara and blasts me with his dimples.

I shake my head. "Another woman bedazzled by your charm."

"I'm here to help." Channing invades my space, taking my work phone and placing it on the countertop before backing me into it. He's shirtless, and the scent of his sweat, clean and manly, makes my core throb.

"It doesn't work on me," I lie.

"You sure about that?" His low rumble goes straight to my core.

I turn away, but now I'm trapped between the kitchen cabinets and his body. Worse, I don't want to move.

"I was handling that just fine without your help."

"I know what your problem is," he purrs in my ear. Why have I let him get so close? His hands come to my shoulders, kneading them. It feels so good, I bite back a moan. "You have control issues."

Of course, he's right. Most lawyers are type A. Organized. Controlling. "I'm a single mom. I have to be on top of things." My argument is weakened by the way my head lolls on my neck, blissfully accepting his massage.

"You need to relax. I can help you with that."

"You're a pain in the ass," I grumble.

"I can be a pain in your ass."

My eyes fly open. His cock is digging into my ass. "What?" I face him, and he looks so innocent.

"What?"

"Back off." I risk putting my hand to his chest to push him away. His skin sears my palm. He takes the tiniest step back. "I don't want your help."

"I'm sorry." He holds up both hands. "I know you've been running the show all by yourself all these years. I totally left you in the lurch. You've done an amazing job. But I'm here now and want to help. But wouldn't it be nice to relax and let someone else take over?" I close my eyes to put some space between us, but his deep voice rumbles through me. "It'd be so easy. Just lie back and let me do all the work."

Images fill my head—ones from my dream, from seeing Channing naked, and more, new images of me in every position, obeying his every command.

"Relax, Julia," he whispers, and I do, inhaling his scent.

I hear him suck in a ragged breath, like he's as turned on as I am. Possibly as bothered by it as I am.

I feel the barest touch of his fingertips brushing my hair from my face.

"I'm sorry," he murmurs again. "I never meant to hurt you by staying away. I didn't realize...I mattered that much."

I open my eyes and find his gorgeous face blurry, obscured by my unshed tears. "Of course you mattered, Channing. You were part of our family. My family. You're Geo's uncle. I loved you like my own brother."

The moment I say it, I know my mistake.

The vulnerability in Channing's face morphs to that impassive, battle face I saw out on the deck last night.

And that's when I realize this attraction definitely isn't one-sided. Channing feels it, too. I haven't been imagining things.

And I just inadvertently shut it all down by saying I felt brotherly toward him.

He gives me a tight, dimpleless smile and moves away, and I'm left alone, aching for what I just turned away.

I twist the wedding band on my finger. Look down at it.

Am I ready to move on? It's been years since I've been with a man. After having a man like Geoffrey—*a shifter*—ordinary human men were just not even the slightest bit interesting to me.

Channing isn't an ordinary human man, though. He's all shifter. All male. He makes my pulse race and my blood heat. I can't deny that since the moment he showed up on my drive, I've been imagining what it would be like to be with him.

If there was anyone on this planet who might fulfill the neediness in me, the emptiness, I think it might be Channing.

I slide the ring off, stare at my finger without it, then slip it back on.

I don't know. Moving on is scarier than holding onto the ache of the past.

I listen for the sounds of Channing moving around the house, checking locks, putting things away, and I realize the ache of the past has already morphed into something else.

Longing.

Longing for my future.

Chapter Seven

Channing

For two days, I keep my head down and do everything I can to help around the house. I fixed the roof. Today I'm sanding the deck and chairs. Tomorrow I will stain and seal them. Julia's car needs an oil change and a thorough check up. Buddy is coming with his tools to help me with that.

And all the while, I remind myself that Julia loves me *like a brother*.

So awesome. That will make it much easier to leave again once I'm sure Geo's comfortable with shifting.

I remind myself of that fact thirty times a day to keep from touching her. Brother. Brother. Brother. Just her brother. I'm using everything I can to keep from marking her with my teeth. Keep from betraying my brother's memory by claiming his mate.

Why would Fate make us both fall for the same human female? I've heard of some unusual shifter packs where the males mate in pairs–but never brothers. And they're a slightly different species of wolf.

It is interesting to note that I didn't have the urge to mark her until Geoffrey died. I thought she was hot. Enjoyed hanging around her. But it wasn't until his funeral that the urge to mark her and claim her hit. As if Fate threw me in as a substitute. But I was only nineteen. I was partying a lot, hanging out with Buddy. Working at a local pizza joint and racing cars on the side for money. Basically, doing nothing with my life.

Julia was ten years older. A lawyer. Out of my league. And she was grieving for my brother. I knew I wasn't fit to fill his shoes. Not even close. I never will be.

So I joined the military–to remove myself from the temptation of Julia and to grow up. I guess, subconsciously, I chose to mold myself after Geoffrey and make myself worthy of her. Except I quickly learned, I couldn't be Geoffrey. I'm not serious and determined. I'm a goofball. I roll with things. Go with the flow. Love to laugh. I've never had any desire to lead. I'm a great soldier.

And then I was recruited to Colonel Johnson's Shifter Op team–he was the same guy who recruited Geoffrey. And… the years went by. It was easier to stay away than to show up and risk sullying my brother's memory by seducing his mate.

Julia certainly didn't need me confusing matters.

I had no idea she was hurt by my absence. That she would've wanted me around.

But *as a brother*. As an uncle to Geo.

Not as a mate.

Alpha's Command

I walk into the living room to find Julia on a yoga mat, her ass in the air. I don't know why she's not working right now. Some kind of break?

All I know is she's killing me.

I swear to fate, she's been purposely trying to tempt me since that day she told me she loved me as a brother. Walking around in a short, silky robe at night. Moaning when she's alone in her bed.

I heard her vibrator going last night and nearly beat down the door to get to her.

All I can say is, thank Fate Geo needs to run in the woods every night because it's the only thing that helps me keep the edge off.

Right now, she's in a bra top and tight little shorts. Her toned legs look amazing, and her ass...

Aw, fuck.

I can't stop the low growl that comes rocketing out of my mouth when she pushes that ass back toward me. She walks her hands backward toward her feet and holds onto her ankles, looking through her legs at me.

That's when I see it. Or rather, don't see it. The wedding band is gone from her finger.

Oh, fuck.

"Hey, Channing." Her voice sounds throaty. Sexy as hell.

I sprout a chub. "What"--I clear my throat– "What are you doing?"

"Yoga. What's it look like?"

I can't stop myself from prowling closer. Far too close. "Need help?" I shouldn't have said it.

Brotherly.

Loves me *like a brother*.

But she took the ring off. Maybe she's just cleaning it? Or was putting on lotion? Maybe she doesn't wear it when she does yoga?

"No." She flows through some more poses, then lingers in the same position, with her ass turned back toward me.

I reach for her hips without even knowing I'm going to do it. My hands grip the sides of her pelvis, another growl erupting from my lips.

I expect Julia to get pissed. Maybe kick me in the face.

Instead, she freezes. Like she's waiting to see what I'll do next.

I need to back the fuck off. Get my hands off my brother's mate. I force myself to release her and take a step back.

She stands and turns, her cheeks flushed from being upside down.

"Can you lift your leg above your head?" I go for light and flirty. My playboy persona.

"Why?"

"Could come in handy." I wink and turn to walk away.

I scent her arousal before I do, and it takes everything in me not to whirl, pick her up and carry her to her bedroom. Or better yet, drop to that yoga mat and...

Nope. Not happening.

Except, why not? She may *say* she loves me as a brother, but her body is responding to mine. Maybe I just need to give her a little pleasure. Get her to shift her perspective of me.

Oh. Fuck me.

From her bedroom, I hear the sound of that damn vibrator again. A tiny whimper.

I can't help it. I'm reaching for her bedroom doorknob before I've even decided to move. And once inside...I can't stop myself.

Julia's on her back, the vibrator shoved inside the yoga shorts to get at her clit, her eyes wild.

I force myself to walk slowly. Not to take a flying leap to land on the bed and cover her body with my own.

She locks gazes with me as she works the tool between her legs, and I know my eyes must change color because I can feel the heat and prickle of the Change trying to come over me. My wolf wants to mark her. I haven't even kissed her yet, and he's ready.

"Now, can I help?" My voice is sandpaper.

She sucks in a ragged breath but doesn't answer. Just keeps those dark eyes fixed on mine. Holds the vibrator still as her hips buck against it.

The room spins. My cock is harder than marble.

"What are you thinking of?"

She pants. "Nothing..."

"Try again. Julia, what are you thinking about when you pleasure yourself?"

She stops moving.

"Don't stop," I command. I don't mean to, but some of that alpha command infuses my voice, and she goes at it with wanton need, throwing her head back and moaning as she grinds her hips over the wand.

"You," she whispers, voice hoarse. "I was thinking of you."

Satisfaction flows through me from head to dick. I'm pretty desperate to get between her legs and finish the job, but I also don't want to change a single thing about this moment. About seeing Julia like this, wild and abandoned, desperate to get off while she thinks of me.

"Good girl."

Her hips judder as if my praise is enough to make her come.

"Keep touching." The alpha command shimmers in the syllables. Humans don't usually respond to it the way wolves do, but apparently Julia finds it sexy. She must like a little domination in the bedroom.

I stand at the foot of her bed, gaze intent on my beautiful female.

I reach for her yoga shorts and tug them off, so I can see the place between her legs.

She's making needy sounds in her throat now. Keening and whining. Desperation to come soaks every syllable.

"That's it, Jewels. Show me how you get your pleasure but don't come."

She whimpers.

"I know you're ready, but I'm still enjoying the show. You look so beautiful when you let go."

She moans some more.

"Slide your hand up to your breast." Keeping one hand securely on the vibrator, she brings the other one inside her yoga bra and squeezes her own breast.

"Pinch your nipple. Show me how stiff you can get it, beautiful."

She bucks her hips and sobs as her fingers pinch the nipple.

I unfasten the front clasp of the yoga bra so it flaps open, releasing her breasts. I lower my head and suck the other nipple while she continues to pleasure herself, fingers working her nipple, wand between her legs.

I take over with the wand, taking it from her and pressing it inside her, seeking her G-spot with the tip. "Use your fingers on that clit," I command.

She rubs and circles it, her belly shuddering in and out with her sobbing breaths. "Please...Channing. I have to come."

Oh, fuck me. How many thousands of times have I fantasized about this moment? About Julia begging me to come in that sweet as honey voice of hers? That lilac and lavender scent mingling with her arousal to make the most magical scent on Earth?

I kiss the stretch marks on her belly. Flick my tongue inside her belly button. Then I capture her fingers and move them aside, so I can suck her stiffened clit. I torture her for a solid thirty seconds, thrusting the vibrator in and out as I suck and flick her clit and she pinches both nipples.

I lift my head. "Now, Julia. Come for me, sweetness."

She screams. Her hips lift off the bed and knees slap my shoulders, and she releases in a wild spasmodic bucking.

I nearly weep from the sight, it's so beautiful. So long in arriving. So perfect.

Julia, coming for me.

Not mine, yet, but giving herself to me.

Allowing me to witness her pleasure. To participate.

I want to profess my love. To tell her how long I've wanted her. How much she means to me, but I'm not good with that sort of thing. I'm the guy who cracks the jokes and lightens the mood. Not the one who gets serious and bares his soul.

So I settle for stroking my hands all over her body, touching her skin. Worshiping. Showing her with my actions, my touch, what she means to me.

"Well." She pushes up to her forearms, breathless. Beautiful.

"I'm going to be helping out *a lot more* around here," I promise with mock sincerity.

A laugh bubbles up and bursts from her lips. She grabs a pillow and flings it at me. "*Channing.*" She's laughing and exasperated.

I played it all wrong.

"Get out." There's a smile on her face, but she points at the door.

Not wanting to push my luck, I drop one more kiss on the flat of her belly and back off the bed.

"A *lot* more," I reiterate as I walk backward toward the door.

Her smile is pure sunshine and warm earth. But she shakes her head as if I'm still the incorrigible teen coming in from the night at six a.m. and waking Geo too early.

I leave her room and close the door, leaning back against it for a moment, committing every detail of the scene to memory before I return to my sanding work outside.

* * *

Julia

Amazing how different an orgasm with another person is

compared to those I achieve on my own. And Channing wasn't even inside me.

I shower and crack a window because I'm not sure how intelligent Geo's sense of smell is now, I don't want him knowing I fooled around with Channing while he was at school.

I don't even know how I feel about what just happened between us, much less how to frame it to my son.

Oh hey, I decided to screw your uncle. That's not weird, is it?

Not that I actually screwed him. But, I definitely want more. So. Much. More.

Except I can't tease out all the threads of panicked thoughts about this development.

I mean, I'm not really the type to just roll with things. I think and overthink. And my thoughts all lead me to this being a bad idea. I know sex with Channing would be amazing, but I'm not really the type who can separate sex from love.

And I can't open my heart to a guy who's going to blast out of here in another five minutes and stay away for ten more years. I definitely can't open my heart to a guy who's involved in risky missions that involve shooting drug dealers, blowing up things, and whatever else he's been doing for hire.

That's not even taking into consideration the fact that he's ten years younger than I am and is my dead husband's brother!

Strangely enough, it doesn't feel disloyal to Geoffrey, though. Being with Channing feels more like an honoring of him. Channing was a part of our life together. Geoffrey loved Channing deeply. I did, too, but in a different way than now.

Now, I see him as a man. A gorgeous, capable and extremely attentive man. One my body craves almost as much as my lonely heart does.

I took off my wedding ring this morning and put it away in my jewelry box. Some day, maybe Geo can give it to his mate. I do recognize it's time for me to move on, whether it's just allowing myself to have pleasure with another man or something more.

I get through the rest of my work day, emerging an hour after Geo gets home from school to find Channing standing outside hosing himself down with his shirt off. *Again.*

I watch through the kitchen window as he stands talking to Geo, water running in rivulets down his sculpted muscles.

Good Lord–will this man ever wear clothing? He's torturing me!

Of course, I have to admit to torturing him a bit, too, with that yoga thing. I saw I'd struck a nerve with the brother comment, and, well, I guess I didn't like the direction things had gone afterward.

Having Channing around makes me feel beautiful again. Seen. Desirable.

He looks up and our gazes lock. I expected awkwardness after what just happened. I was going to push him away, so I could come up for air. But there's so much dark promise in his green gaze that my knees go weak.

Who knew? The lackadaisical goof has an intense side. And, apparently, a semi-responsible side, judging by the way he's helping around the house and mentoring Geo.

And that's the moment it happens. Despite my better judgment. Despite my reluctance. The gates to my heart pop open and a flood of affection rushes out to meet Channing.

He must see it in my expression because his chin lifts and hope blooms in his slow, sexy smile.

Hope.

For me?

Can that actually be the case? My head spins.

I don't know what's happening here. Is Channing trying to seduce me?

No, no. That's crazy. He came because Geo hit puberty, and he was finally stepping up to his responsibilities as an uncle. I need to remind myself that this man is not to be relied upon.

He's not Geoffrey, no matter how much he may remind me of him.

Still, I'm beginning to enjoy having him here. And my body is alive again.

I put some rice in the cooker and turn the oven on to roast a chicken. It probably won't be enough meat for my wolves, but I can always crack open one of the many packs of hotdogs they had delivered if they need a second dinner after their run.

I move through the kitchen, humming, surprised by how relaxed I feel. It's not just the orgasm—or maybe it is. But it's also having Channing here.

Things feel different. Two people didn't really make a family. Everything fell on my shoulders. It was exhausting. As much as I resisted it, it's nice to have someone else in the house to pick up the slack.

I don't know how long he'll stay, but I might as well enjoy it while he's here. Staycation. I can live with that.

Channing and Geo come in through the back door. Channing's jeans are wet from his hose-down and hang below his waist, so I have a clear view of the V of muscles that lead to the promised land.

He catches me looking and winks.

Damn him.

I don't want to surrender to that charm. I need to guard myself against whatever this is.

"I'm going to shower." He jerks his thumb toward the bathroom, and I push away the desire to follow him. "Geo has a little homework to finish before we can run." He glances at Geo and tips his head toward the stairs. "Get to it."

"'Kay." Geo takes them two at a time. No trace of surliness or slouchiness. He's all in on whatever Channing says, it seems.

"Dinner will be ready in about forty-five minutes," I tell him. Wow. Just like a real family. It feels so good, it makes my chest squeeze.

Channing's dimples deepen. "Perfect. I'll get cleaned up and come and help you."

I pour myself a glass of wine and make a salad. When Channing comes out of the bathroom, he sets the table and pours his own glass of wine.

I prop a hip against the counter and watch him.

"Cheers." He clinks glasses lightly with mine, stepping into my space. Invading my sanity.

I study him. I have to ask. "Why did you stay away so

long?" I'm able to say it without it sounding like an accusation. Without resentment.

I just really want to know.

Pain contorts his beautiful face. The same pain I saw when Geoffrey died. He drops his head, staring at the floor between us.

"Was it too painful?" I ask softly. "It reminded you too much of Geoffrey?"

When Channing looks up, he's blinking hard. "No." He shakes his head. "It wasn't that. It was painful, but—"

I wait for him to go on, but he doesn't. He looks out the darkening window, his eyes glowing slightly, telling me he can see in the twilight far better than I.

"But what?"

"I wanted to be there for you," he croaks.

"So why weren't you?" This time, my voice cracks—I can't help some of the emotion returning. Some of my resentment. "We needed you, Channing."

"You needed Geoffrey," he says gruffly—a tone I'm not used to hearing from him. "You needed a man. Someone who could protect and care for you. Someone responsible. I wasnt that man, Julia. So I left. I went to become the man Geoffrey was."

I cock my head, eyes narrowing in confusion. "I didn't need you to be Geoffrey. I just needed my family." Tears spear my eyes. The hurt beneath my resentment coming up to be expressed. "You don't understand. We were in mourning... I lost my husband and my son's father. And then I lost you too! My only solace while I was grieving him was that at least Geo would have an uncle. And then we lost you *both*. What did we do to deserve your rejection?"

"Julia," Channing chokes. His own eyes look damp. "I couldn't stay. You don't understand."

I slap his chest. "Explain it to me!"

"Because I'm a fuck-up, Julia. I didn't want to fuck up your lives, too."

I shake my head. None of this makes sense. "How could you possibly?"

Channing shoves his hands in his pockets, a gesture that makes him look more like that wayward teen I remember. "It was the day of the funeral. The casket hadn't even been lowered in the ground when..." He trails off, working to swallow.

"When what?"

"My wolf..." He sucks in a breath like there's not enough air in the room. "My wolf made it clear that he wanted to claim you."

I draw back in shock. Blink, trying to absorb what that means. "What?" My hand goes to my outer thigh–the place Geoffrey marked me with his scent the night he claimed me. The scars are still there–more permanent than the simple wedding band I took off. Geoffrey's scent is still there, telling other wolves I've been claimed.

Channing gives a miserable shrug. "You were my brother's fated mate...and also mine." His eyes glow green when he stares at me.

My wine glass slips from my fingers, and he catches it with lightning reflexes, splattering us both with the red zinfandel.

"Oh God!" I'm happy for the distraction. For the chance to organize my thoughts. "I'm sorry." I grab the dish towel and press it against his stained white t-shirt.

"Julia." He takes the towel from me and sets it on the counter. When he cradles my head with both hands, there's nothing boyish about him.

He's all man now.

My panties dampen. The flesh between my legs squeezes.

"Now do you understand? Why I left and stayed away? Why I was afraid to come back?"

My breathing has grown erratic. Wild. I'm mesmerized by his glowing green gaze. The intensity of his focus on me. "What were you afraid of?" I whisper.

"This." He lowers his head and kisses me. It's a passionate kiss, filled with love and need and the promise of pleasure. His lips move over mine, claiming my mouth, stroking it. Tasting it. His tongue slides along the seam, pressing in, bold but respectful. Slow enough for me to refuse if I wanted to.

I don't.

I've never wanted to be kissed so badly in my life.

Never wanted to give myself to someone. Never felt so treasured.

All this time, he waited for me.

Channing Armstrong. Pining for me.

Denying himself this pleasure of me.

Growing up for me.

I feel the importance of it in the wood floor under my

feet. In the shake and tremble of the trees outside the window. In the walls of the house.

Geoffrey was wonderful. Geoffrey was hot, and dominant, and manly.

Channing is all of those things, but with a legacy of pain and wanting that spans years. He tortured himself over me.

I know what it means for a wolf to have an unclaimed mate. I know it can kill some males. They go moon mad.

Channing nearly killed himself for me.

So I reach for his head, and I kiss him back. Kiss him until we both grow feverish, and he picks me up by the waist and sits me on the counter. Spreads my knees to stand between them and slide his hands up my shirt.

And that's when Geo comes running down the stairs.

Channing jerks away from me and rubs his mouth with his hand as he turns to face Geo, who stares at us both with wide eyes.

I find my voice. "All done with your homework?"

Chapter Eight

Channing

Guilt shades my run with Geo. I'm not sure whether I'm guilty over not being here all along for him or for showing up out of the blue and wanting to claim his mom. I haven't acted with integrity, and I want to punch my own face over it.

We both played it off in the kitchen like I hadn't just been about to push his mom back on the counter and feast between her legs until she screamed her throat raw.

It's Friday night, so we run extra long, stopping at the ridge to practice shifting. I teach him how to track a deer and stop him from following the bobcat whose scent he caught. Of course, he could win a fight with a bobcat, but there's no reason to hunt another predator.

After the run, we shift and dress and eat a second dinner on the freshly-sanded deck. It's late and the house is dark. Julia's already gone to bed.

When we finish, we sit in relaxed companionship.

"I, uh..." I clear my throat. "I should tell you about shifter mating."

"That's okay," Geo says quickly. Because what kid wants to have the sex talk with an adult he barely knows and who's macking on his mom?

"Wolves mate for life. Shifter wolves have fated mates. The one mate intended by nature as the perfect match."

Geo stops pretending to ignore me and swivels his head to meet my gaze.

I give a nod. "Some wolves never find their fated mate. They mate anyway, raise families and can live in total happiness."

He continues to watch me, perhaps waiting for me to get to the point.

"If or when you meet your fated mate, you'll know, because you'll have the urge to mark her."

Geo's forehead scrunches in confusion.

"Your fangs will come down coated with a serum unique to you. You'll bite her and permanently embed your scent into her flesh, so every other male will know she's been marked and belongs to you."

Geo draws back in shock.

I plunge forward because it's important Geo understand these things. He's a wolf. Some day, I hope he will find his own fated mate.

"Your mom... she was your dad's fated mate."

"Your brother."

"That's right."

"What about you?" His eyes catch the moonlight. I

already love this kid so much. I don't know how I could have ever stayed away.

I clear my throat. "Your mom is also my fated mate. That's why I stayed away. I found out right after your dad died, and it was too soon. Your mom needed time to grieve, and I needed to grow up."

"How old were you?"

"Nineteen."

He bobs his head, absorbing all this without much expression. "So you're going to mark my mom? Or you already have?" He scrunches up his face with disgust. "Nevermind—I don't want to know."

I give him an affectionate smile. "Your mom hasn't even forgiven me for staying away so long. But if it happens, you'll know." I touch my nose.

"Right. I'll smell it. Gross."

My grin widens. "It's not gross. It's wolf nature. It's our form of a wedding ring."

Geo loops his long, lanky arms around his knees. "Cool."

"Is it, bud?"

He shrugs. "Yeah."

"I didn't...I never felt worthy of stepping into my brother's shoes. I know I can't do that. But...I'm here for you, Geo. No matter what happens between me and your mom, you can depend on me. I want you to know that." I fight to swallow down the lump in my throat. This is so much bigger than my intense attraction to Julia. This is about Geo. And the promise I made my brother. "You're my blood. My family. My pack."

Geo climbs to his feet like I didn't just bare my soul–

admit the thing I've been avoiding for the past ten years. "Cool. I'm going to bed."

"Good night, Junior."

"Night."

I climb to my feet and go to wash up. Julia appears in the open doorway of the bathroom wearing a pair of miniscule sleep shorts and a thin tank top. She rests her hands on either side of the door frame, causing her breasts to lift and separate, shifting beneath the thin fabric of her nightshirt. It's a clear invitation, and it's all I can do to stop from claiming her right where she stands.

She sucks in a sharp breath, probably noticing the change in color of my irises.

"Looks like you might need my help again," I rumble.

A sultry smile curves her lips. "I do."

* * *

Julia

Channing crooks a finger at me, and I walk forward, dropping my arms to my sides. As soon as I'm within reaching distance, he settles his hands on my waist.

It feels so good to be touched again.

I didn't realize how badly I needed this.

I honestly don't know what's going to happen between me and Channing. He's done his share of shocking me. Disappearing. Staying away for ten years. Reappearing and claiming I'm his mate.

I'm having a hard time reconciling it all. I think I need to

Alpha's Command

just forget the young man who left here so long ago and just get to know this Channing.

The grown-up, dominant in the bedroom, nurturing to my son, Channing.

A guy I really don't know.

We need a complete restart.

He picks me up, spins and sits me on the bathroom counter.

"Now, where were we?" he rumbles, stepping between my legs, and pulling my tank top off in a smooth movement. My nipples harden under his heated gaze. He brushes his thumbs over the peaked tips as he nibbles my ear.

I fist his t-shirt. "*Now* you're wearing a shirt," I complain. "The one time I wish you weren't."

He reaches behind his head to pull it off with one hand in one elegant move. "Happy to fix that problem." He kisses down my neck as I coast my palms over his golden chest.

This guy has probably been with hundreds of women, and my number is three. Total. Two before Geoffrey and no one since. Getting intimate with someone after such a long stint alone and basically only one man for the years before that is... a little awkward.

I don't even know if I"m good at this. If I remember how.

Geoffrey was so dominant, he took charge in the bedroom. Channing is a little more respectful. Or maybe he's just holding back.

I trace the ridges of his abs with a fingertip. "It's...it's a lot to take in—you. Me. This."

He cradles my face and lifts it to his. "I know." He

brushes his lips over mine, exploring softly. Nibbles. Tastes me. "We can go slowly. Get used to each other. See if you can stand me." He flashes his most charming grin and my insides flutter.

I wrap my legs around his waist and tug hips forward.

"I can stand you," I whisper.

He hooks his forearm behind my butt and lifts me from the counter to carry me into the bedroom.

When he lays me on my back in the center of the bed, I get nervous. "It's, um, been a long time for me," I admit.

Channing strokes a palm between my breasts and down my once-taut belly. Now the skin is too loose and the stretch marks are still present from my pregnancy fourteen years ago.

"I'll go slow," Channing promises. He tugs my shorts off and groans when he sees I shaved this afternoon.

"Was this for me?" He kisses my mons, strokes the pad of his thumb lightly over my slit, not parting me yet, just titillating me with a feather touch. Moisture gathers at my entrance.

My internal muscles squeeze, and I shiver. "Well, I don't know what the fashion is these days and—"

He stops me with a finger on my lips. "It's perfect. I fucking love it. So pretty." As if to prove it, he pushes my knees wide and kneels between my legs, biting and kissing up my inner thigh.

I let out a warbling breath. He puts my knee over his shoulder and licks into me, tracing the inside of my labia with the tip of his tongue. I squeeze and buck, pushing against his mouth for more.

"Uh uh. Bad girl. You're not in charge here." Channing catches my wrists and pins them to my sides.

Oh God. Channing the goofball is ridiculous but loveable. But Channing the dominant lover? I go dizzy with desire. My pussy floods with moisture, my skin grows feverish.

Channing notices. He lifts his head to give me a satisfied smirk. "You want to have someone take the control away from you, don't you, Jewels? So you can let go and enjoy for once?" He lowers his head and swirls his tongue around my clit.

Do I? My first instinct is to deny it. I need control. It helps me feel safe and capable and organized. That's how I got through law school. How I raised a child as a single working mom.

But there's no denying my body's response to having my hands pinned to my sides. To knowing Channing's going to do whatever he wants between my legs, and it's not up to me how or when I orgasm.

Maybe it helps with my nerves, too. With the awkwardness of intimacy after such a dry spell. I don't have to perform, I just have to let Channing take control.

"Should I tie you up, Jewels?" He lifts his head once more, his eyes glowing green in the darkness. "Yes, I think you need to be restrained."

I lick my lips, more excited than I could have ever imagined. Channing tugs my wrists over my head, pinning them together.

"Don't move." He does that trick of his, making his command reverberate through my entire body.

An orgasm rips through me. Just like that–no physical contact. Just his deep, growly voice.

Channing's brows pop, and he pulls a mock-stern face. "Did you just come?"

My head lolls on my neck, my brain short-circuiting with the unexpected release. "No...I mean, yes. Oh my God."

"Did I *say* you could come?"

I let out a breathy laugh. Is that how we're playing this? I'm dying.

I adore this Channing. My entire body is alive. Vibrating. Desperate for every depraved thing he wants to do with me.

"Sorry, not sorry," I laugh as he stalks to my dresser and yanks open a drawer.

He returns with a knee-high sock of mine, which he uses to tie my wrists together.

"Not sorry? You might wanna rethink that answer." He rolls me to my belly and slaps my ass, hard enough to make me jump and squeal.

"Ouch." I laugh and wiggle for more.

He delivers three more sharp spanks, then slides his fingers between my legs. I'm so wet and ready that his fingers sink into my entrance, guided by my plumped flesh.

"Hmm, you like a little punishment, too. I'm finding out all kinds of things I didn't know about you." His thumb slides in the cleft of my ass, settling on my back entrance as he nips my shoulder.

I gasp, squeezing at the sensation. The beyond-intimate touch revs my engine even more, even as I squirm to get away.

Alpha's Command

"Uh uh." Channing scolds, applying pressure to my anus as his fingers arc in and out of my sopping entrance.

I'm ready to come again. I don't know if it's because it's been so long since I've been with a partner or–

No, it's Channing.

He's a master at this, and my body responds like it belongs to him.

With my arms tied above my head, my face is pressed into the bedcovers. I bite at the comforter, rolling and bucking my hips.

"I'm going to come again," I warn him.

"No, you're not." He uses the voice. It makes everything tingle below my waist.

"Please, Channing."

He continues to explore my wet channel as he massages my back hole. "Mmm. I like it when you beg."

"Please. Oh God, please."

"What do you need, Jewels?"

I want him deeper. Or more on my clit. Or for him just to give me permission... Wait, am I actually waiting for permission to orgasm? Me? The control freak?

Yes, I guess I am. I've completely surrendered control to Channing, and it feels wonderful. Floaty and free. Even while I'm lightheaded with lust.

"More," I croon. "I need more."

Channing's fingers slip out of my wet channel and sweep over my clit. A shudder runs through me. I'm so close.

But he's still not giving me what I want. What I need.

"I need to come," I plead. "Please, Channing."

And then I arrive at what I really need. What my body desperately craves.

"I need you."

Channing's growl of satisfaction blasts through the room. He withdraws his fingers and slaps my ass. A warning, perhaps, that asking for him will mean it will get rough. Rowdy.

I can't wait to experience Channing's full dominance. To see what happens when the charming, laid-back Channing falls away, and I glimpse the predator behind those dimples.

I hear the rustle of clothes as he shucks his jeans, and then he climbs up over me. "I'm wearing protection," he says, and I hear the rip of a foil package as he opens a condom.

"Spread your legs," Julia. He uses the Alpha Command. At least, I think that's what it is. That particular timbre of voice that makes my body weak with surrender. Wet with desire.

I part my legs. My nipples chafe against the comforter. My arms are still stretched taut above my head.

"Good girl." The warm rumble sends shivers through me.

"Please," I whimper. I'm not above begging now.

Channing squeezes my ass with both hands, his touch rough and possessive. He separates my cheeks and doesn't move for a moment, like he's drinking in the sight of me open and exposed to him.

"So fucking pretty," he growls.

The reservations I had earlier, the worries I had about the state of my almost-40, post child-bearing body, or about my ability to get intimate with someone new, they all evaporate.

Channing makes me feel beautiful.

I lift my hips in invitation, arch my lower back even more.

"I'm going to fuck that pretty ass soon," Channing vows as he nudges my legs wider and brings his cock between my legs.

"Yes," I practically wail the moment he rubs the head over my slick juices.

"You need me here?" He continues the teasing, not entering me, just rubbing over my slit.

"Yes."

He shoves into me with one glorious, satisfying thrust.

"*God*, yes." He's thick and long and too much but so perfect.

"Is that what you needed, Julia? A long, rough ride on my cock?"

I'm stretched wide with him, plowed open. This union of our bodies, this coupling feels vital and necessary. Like this was the one thing I've been missing my whole life. "Yes. Channing."

He pauses, and I nearly die. Then he shoves in deep and hard with a snap of his hips. "Say it again." His voice is pure sandpaper.

"Yes," I say, then realize what he means. "*Channing*. Yes, Channing."

"Whose cock do you need?" Another brutal thrust and a stop.

"Yours. Please."

And then Channing comes undone. I hear his rough exhale as he braces one fist beside my head and grips my nape, holding me down like I'm his sex doll. "I'll give you what you need, Julia."

He thrusts into me, finding an orgasm-worthy rhythm—hard enough, fast enough. Rough enough.

I could go off any second, but I wait.

"Channing...Channing," I chant.

Every time I say his name, he lets out a groan. Like it physically affects him to hear it.

"You need to come, Julia?" His voice is so deep, so animalistic, I can barely understand the words.

"Yes," I sob. I'm desperate. But I also don't want this to be over. It's so good.

Everything I didn't know I needed.

Channing pulls out, and I whimper with disappointment. He rolls me to my back.

I reach for him with my bound hands, but he pins them back down against the bed as he climbs over me.

"I wanna see your face when you come, Beautiful. But not until I say. Understand?"

"Yes." *No.* I don't understand, but I would say anything right now to get the release I need.

"Good girl."

I would say anything for another *good girl* from Channing. I'm not the type of person to need approval, but every time he says it, a flame lights me, warms me from the inside.

Channing lifts my legs to put my ankles over his broad, muscular shoulders. He lines the head of his cock up with my entrance and thrusts in.

"Yes!" I cry out. The brief absence of having him inside

me makes it all the more incredible and satisfying now. "Please, Channing."

"Not yet, Jewels." There's command in his voice. It lights every nerve ending in my body. Seeps into my bones.

Claims me.

His *voice* claims me.

If this is what it feels like to be claimed by the timbre of his voice, what would it be like to be fully claimed by him?

But no, I'm not ready for that. It's too much to contemplate.

My thoughts scramble away, loosened by the delicious weight of Channing's hand pinning my wrists, of his hips snapping against mine. Of his big, glorious cock sliding in and out of me.

"More," I plead, even though he's already slapping into me hard and fast.

He pushes my legs back to my shoulders, so I'm in plow position, and he rises over me, bottoming out with each thrust now. "Love that yoga," he growls. There's no wink or flash of his dimples. He's too far gone for that.

And I love seeing him this way. In the throes of passion. For me. Channing undone over me.

He slows down, rolls me to my side and pushes one knee up toward my chest, taking me in this position. The angle is delicious and so is the contact of Channing molded against my back, one powerful hand gripping the back of my thigh with bruising force.

Channing's breath grows ragged. He thrusts with more force.

"Channing..."

"Say it again." He's panting. His words are ragged. Syllables broken.

"Channing."

"One more time."

"Channing."

His thrusts are wild and rough. His cock is searing hot. "Come for me, Julia." He shoves in and stays, bucking his hips against me as he violently releases.

I squeeze and grip his cock with my internal muscles. Shudder and shake with wave after wave of well-earned pleasure.

"Channing," I murmur one more time as he gentles his thrusts, sliding his hand up to squeeze my breast as we work through the aftershocks together. Wring out every last quake and tremble.

* * *

Channing

I ease out and toss the condom in the trashcan near the bed then pull Julia into my arms.

I'm not a cuddler. I'm not a wham-bam-thank-you-ma'am type, either. I'm respectful. Give a woman what she needs. Charm the hell out of her before I leave.

But holding Julia after sex is a fucking *honor*.

A life purpose.

More than I deserve. Everything I crave.

Not marking her during sex was a fucking torment, but I kept my jaw locked. Kept my fangs from scoring her delicate human flesh.

She's not mine to claim.

In my mind, and I'm sure, in hers, she still belongs to Geoffrey. Knowing that, I can't get over the guilt and inadequacy wanting to claim her evokes in me.

Still, I can give her pleasure. I can ease her burden while I'm here. Give Geo the guidance he needs.

I won't stay away so long again. Hell, I could make the drive to Flagstaff from Taos every week if she wanted me to. But pushing in on Geoffrey's territory–marking her as my own–that wouldn't be right.

More than that–I'm sure it wouldn't be welcome.

She's only just barely forgiving me for fucking up as an uncle.

"This feels so strange," she murmurs, her lips soft against my chest.

"I know," I say. I gather from her confession that it has been a long time, that she hasn't been with anyone since Geoffrey.

Part of me feels like an asshole for intruding on that loyalty. But she deserves pleasure. She deserves a male to lean on. Partnership. Even if it doesn't come in as honorable and worthy a package as Geoffrey.

I'm not even going to say I'm the next best thing because I'm a far cry from Geoffrey. Every male in my pack is probably more worthy of a female like Julia than I am. But I'm the guy who's here. The one who would kill or die for her.

Who would do anything to protect her and Geo.

I kiss her hair, breathing in her lavender and lilac scent.

"Strange but good," she says, and my heart gives a double-pump.

"So good." I somehow manage to keep my voice steady.

My wolf nudges me to take this further, but I ignore him. For now, this is enough. My mate is here in my arms. Naked. Sated. Well-loved.

Not claimed, but that can wait.

I'd wait an entire lifetime for this female.

Chapter Nine

Julia

On Tuesday, I wake before Channing and wrap myself in a warm robe. Not wanting to wake anyone, I slip my feet into my house shoes and step outside on the deck to witness dawn.

Today is the anniversary of Geoffrey's death. I don't know if Channing remembers. Geo won't. I don't usually make a big deal out of it.

For the past four days, Channing has turned my world upside down. In a good way. He makes me coffee in the mornings, gets Geo off to school. He invited over his shifter friend, Buddy, and together they've knocked out all the little house projects that have accumulated over the years.

Buddy is a strange character, a huge guy who drives a run down old Charger. His hair is thick black except for white streak right on the center. I want to know what shifter he is, but I'm not sure if it's polite to ask. When I met him, he blinked at me sleepily and said not a word, just quietly helped Channing replace all the windows in the house.

"He's not a big talker," Channing told me later. "But he's the best at surveillance."

"You used him to keep an eye on us?"

Channing gave me a secret smile. I protest, but deep down, I love that he went to such lengths to protect us. To care for me.

Channing's fixed every broken thing around the house.

Including my sex life.

That's been the most incredible part. Every night he makes me scream with pleasure. Last night, he kept me on the edge of an orgasm for over an hour before finally giving me the command to come.

I've never climaxed so hard in my life.

He's been great with Geo. Making sure he gets his homework done. Taking him for a run after dusk. He says Geo can shift between his human and wolf form without a hitch now.

Which has me anxious.

Because I don't know if Channing will hang around much longer. He said I'm his mate, but we've had absolutely no discussion about what that means. What he wants.

It's probably too soon, anyway. We're getting to know each other again.

Today, though, everything feels sticky and hard.

I usually spend the anniversary of Geoffrey's death out in nature on a hike. Out in the forest where Geoffrey loved to run. Every year gets both easier and harder. Easier because the grief lessens its hold on me. But harder because his memory fades even more. I don't want to let go of all the little memories and reminders that used to poke and hurt me. I want to keep them forever. To honor everything Geoffrey was to me.

This year, though, I don't know what to think.

Channing is here. I've slept with him. Multiple times.

It feels disloyal to Geoffrey's memory but not entirely wrong.

The door opens quietly behind me, and Channing steps out in nothing but his boxer shorts.

"Hey." The word is soft. Laced with concern.

He remembers, too, then.

He comes and wraps his arms around me from behind. One of his hands is closed.

I pry it open and find Geoffrey's Army tags. "Where did you find these?" I take them from his hand and turn them over. The sight of them gores me right through the middle. The Army is what took him from me.

"I took them when he died. I...needed something of his to remind me of the kind of man I wanted to become." I hear an ocean of pain and regret in Channing's voice.

I press the tags back into his palm. I don't turn around because I'm already so raw. It's easier to speak without eye contact. Joined together but without the added intensity of being face to face.

I watch the sky changing color from shades of gray to pink and orange.

"He'd be so proud of what you made of yourself, Channing."

Channing clears his throat. "I don't know about that."

Now I turn. I have to. Is Channing functioning from some idea that he still doesn't measure up?

And—*oh, God*—have I reinforced that by treating him like the fuck-up he always was when he showed up here this time? A tight band squeezes my lungs.

"Why do you say that?" I demand.

Channing shrugs. "I'm not Geoffrey. I'm not the leader of my team. I'm a sell-out. I left the military to do work-for-hire. I'm still the guy who you'd rather invite to a party than have a serious conversation with."

My throat closes. "Channing...maybe you're not supposed to be Geoffrey. You're supposed to be you."

He closes his eyes and shakes his head.

I take both sides of his face in my hands. "I mean it," I say fiercely enough to make his lids fly open. "You're not Geoffrey. You think differently. Made different choices in your life. But that doesn't mean you're any less brave. Or your heart isn't as good. Or you have less honor." Even as I say it, I can think of the examples where we both know he's fallen short. Where I've blamed him, and it seems he's blamed himself.

"Listen, Channing. I was mad at you for abandoning us, yes. But now I understand that you didn't. You were watching us this whole time. Sending money. Installing security. What else have you done that I don't even know about?" I ask the question on a hunch, hoping he'll land on something.

He lifts his gaze to the forest edge, looking over my shoulder. "I bought that land so Geo could run."

"What?" I whirl and look at the tree line.

He nods.

"*You're* the one who bought up all the land around us?"

"Wolves need space to run. You had it, but I was afraid someone might come and develop that land, so I made sure that couldn't happen."

Tears prick my eyes. I wrap my arms around Channing and lay my cheek against his chest. "You see?" There's a wobble to my voice. "You're a different version of Geoffrey. A younger, more reckless version whose heart has always been intact. He told me you'd be here for us, and you were. I just didn't know it at the time."

Channing massages the back of my head. "He told you I'd be here for you?" His voice is rusty.

I nod. "He left me a letter in the safe. I found it a few months after–" I choke up.

"What..." Channing clears his throat. "What did it say?"

* * *

Channing

Julia takes my hand. "Come here. You can read it for yourself."

She leads me into the bedroom and pulls a folded letter out of the bottom drawer of her jewelry case. I drop the dog tags in the drawer. She should have them.

The letter is on yellow notebook paper–simple and direct, like Geoffrey. The ink on the lined paper is faded now. The edges are tattered and worn as if she's pulled it out and read it at least a hundred times.

My hands shake a little when I reach for it.

Geoffrey was like a father to me. Our real dad was a lazy, selfish prick, and I don't even remember our mom, who took off when I was five. We came from a backwoods pack in Kentucky whose main source of income was anything illegal.

Geoffrey wanted to better himself, so he left and joined the Army. That meant I had little supervision. By the time I was Geo's age, I was definitely running wild. Stealing cars. Setting fires. Helling around. I managed to talk my way out of most of the trouble I got into, but I was failing out of school. When Geoffrey found out, he brought me out to live in Arizona with him, even though he had a new mate and pup. He let me stick around and intrude on their new life together. To remove me from the temptation of trouble and give me a shot at bettering myself.

I barely think about my dad or my pack of origin, but I think of Geoffrey all the time. The lessons he taught me. His protection. The love.

I smooth out the wrinkled paper and skim it. It was meant for Julia. An expression of his love for her and their pup. Regret that he wouldn't be there to care for them. It contains some practical details–passwords and life insurance.

And then there was the section about me.

Trust Channing. He cares as much about you two as I do, and I know he'll always be there for you. He's the only male I would trust to protect and provide for you.

My eyes burn, and I blink hard. A mountain-sized swell of love and grief mixed together bowl through me.

And regret. Because I didn't protect and provide for Julia and Geo in the way they needed.

I thought I was doing the right thing, but, as usual, I fucked it up.

"Julia..." I choke. "I wish I hadn't fucked this up."

"You didn't, Channing." She wraps her arms around my waist and molds her body against mine. "I was hurt because I didn't understand. But you were just a kid yourself. You were grieving, too. You did the best you could. And I love you for it."

I try to swallow but fail. My brain does a mad-dash scramble trying to figure out if she means she loves me like a brother-in-law or something else. Something more.

And it feels wrong to even hope for the latter on the day we're remembering Geoffrey.

But her lilac and lavender scent is up in my nostrils, driving me mad. Besides, I'm long past acting brotherly.

I stroke my hands down Julia's back until they mold around her tight little yoga ass. I squeeze, dragging her hips up against my leg, so she can ride my thigh, grind against it when I kiss down her neck.

"Is this okay?" I murmur because I want to be respectful. She may feel guilty about us today, too.

But her answer becomes obvious when she slides one hand into the waistband of my boxer briefs and sinks her nails into my asscheek.

"Yeah?" I hoist her up, and her legs wrap around my waist, her arms around my neck. She kisses me like she's hungry for it. Like she needs me as badly as I need her.

I drop her on the bed and climb over her, dragging the robe down from her shoulders. She kicks off her slippers, and I shuck my boxers. I'm usually an attentive lover, but my heart is still in my throat, my emotions raw and ragged. I need Julia like I need my next breath.

Before I even mean to, I've thrust inside her, driving to some destination. Some place where Julia and I will both be healed. Of Geoffrey's death. Of losing each other afterward.

She clings to my shoulders, her nails scoring my skin, her ankles hooked behind my back to urge me onward. Forward. Turning both of us inside out with the frantic pace. The needy climb.

"I need you," she gasps as if voicing my own thoughts.

"I'm here. Always, Julia. I'm yours."

There are tears in her eyes, but I can't slow down enough to kiss them away. To ask if she's okay. If she needs something else besides this urgent joining. This necessary communion of two broken but bonded hearts.

Our hips move in concert, hers lifting to meet mine, then lowering with the force of my thrust, then soaring upward again. I have the sense of the entire world narrowing to this moment.

Her face framed by my hands resting on the bed.

Her teary gaze glued to mine. Like we're riding through the eye of a storm together.

"I need this," she pants. "I need you."

Every time she says it, some wounded place inside me heals.

"I need you, too." My fangs lengthen to mark her, but I keep my lips closed. Draw harsh breaths in through my nostrils to stave off the marking instinct.

She comes, her muscles clamping around my dick. My eyes roll back in my head. My balls tighten.

And then I remember I didn't wear protection, so I pull out and come all over her belly. Marking her in a more temporary way.

It's not enough.

Not for my wolf.

I'll have to claim her soon. Either that, or I'll have to leave.

Chapter Ten

Channing

The next evening, my phone buzzes. Buddy and I spent the past few hours working on Julia's car, and we've just come in to wash up and grab a beer. I answer on autopilot and step outside on the deck.

"How's the mission?" Deke asks.

"Good," I say because I don't really want to get into details. Technically, I've done what I came to do: help my nephew through his first shifts until he's confident enough on his own. But every passing minute it becomes more agonizing to consider leaving. How can I, after hearing Julia say she needs me?

But Deke wouldn't be calling to check on me. He doesn't do small talk. "What's up?"

"We have more news about Hannibal."

"Have you found him?"

"Not yet. But there's evidence that he talked to other kids in private chats."

"To lure them to a fight club?" My wolf rises, making my voice a growl. This Hannibal character needs to be stopped.

"Not sure yet. Kylie's still digging into the app. Jackson is, too, from a different angle. He wants to figure out who's funding the app."

My blood runs cold. Jackson King runs an IT and cybersecurity company based in Tucson. If he doesn't know who created the app, then it's not another shifter. Meaning, shifter teens are talking in an unsecured chat room run by humans.

Shifter teens aren't known for their discretion. They could out the whole shifter community with a few posts. "Are humans behind it? Or maybe a leech? Or a dragon?" Vampires and dragons have the billions to fund a startup.

"We don't know yet. At first we thought it was another shifter kid, but the security is too good. Kylie's having trouble hacking it. She will, though. She's trying to get the locations of some of the users, Hannibal included."

My claws are out. I dig them into my palm. "Let me know when you get a lock on Hannibal."

"Will do. Keep an eye out. He might still be in your area."

I hope he is. I'd like to question him personally.

I pocket my phone and head inside just in time to hear Geo ask Julia,

"Mom, can I go to a fight club?"

Oh shit. Julia's head snaps to me as she asks Geo, "A what?"

"A fight club. For shifters. Channing's friends run it. They're having a pop-up one in Flagstaff."

Crap. I raise my hands. "He overheard Buddy and me talking."

She shakes her head at me but keeps her voice gentle, "No, that doesn't sound like a good idea."

"Fine." Geo shrugs. "I'll just go when I'm over eighteen."

Sorry, I mouth to Julia as we take our seats at the table. Julia made pasta and invited Buddy to stick around, since he and I are working on fixing her car.

After four plates of spaghetti, I kick back, balancing my chair on the back two legs. My abs contract with the effort. On the opposite side of the table, Geo does the same, wobbling and holding on to the edge of the table until he achieves the balance. Delight flickers in his eyes.

Julia is less than pleased. "Can you please stop that?"

We both let the front legs come down with a thump.

"Thank you. Did you three have fun today?"

"Oh yeah," Geo says. "Channing's teaching me to drive a car. Hotwire one, too."

Julia's eyebrows creep up. "Excuse me?"

"You never know when you'll be on the run and need a getaway vehicle," Geo repeats my joke word for word.

I wince.

Julia's lips press together in a way that tells me that she's going to take me to task about it later. Another addition to the list of my sins.

"It's like when you were in Bangkok," Geo continues. "On a mission. And those guys were shooting at you."

Julia sucks in a breath.

"That wasn't Bangkok," I say. "And they weren't shooting at us. They just wanted to have a...conversation. With guns."

"I guess you told him about some of your missions." Julia doesn't sound happy.

"At least that time they weren't shooting silver bullets," Geo prattles on. "They can kill a shifter, you know. Like the time in Italy when Rafe got shot—"

"Geo," I mutter and slice a hand across my neck in a *cut it out* gesture.

"Anyway, your job is cool," Geo mumbles and subsides.

"Channing," Julia says. "I don't think learning to drive or hotwire a car are part of the mentoring Geo requires from you."

"Right. Sorry."

She draws in a breath and sighs. "I have to go out of town next week. An overnight trip to New York." She turns to Geo, her tone apologetic. "If I could get out of it, I would."

"A work trip?" I keep my voice casual, but my wolf wants to howl. "With Mr. Van De Butt?"

Geo snickers, and Julia gives me a disparaging look. "Van den Berg," she corrects, as if I'm simply confused.

Buddy keeps his head down, focused on munching through his third plate of food, but I know he's taking in every detail and could repeat it verbatim.

"Geo, I've arranged for you to stay with Justin's family like last time."

"Can't I stay here? With Uncle Channing?"

I meet Julia's gaze and give a subtle nod. Of course, I'm willing. I'd love some man-to-man time with the pup. I've already taught him how to change the oil in Julia's car, and I bought him a razor and shaving cream for the peach fuzz on his upper lip.

"Maybe next time," Julia says.

Ouch.

I shouldn't let it bother me. The fact that she doesn't think I'm dependable enough to stay with Geo. That she doesn't trust me. I get it–I'm not the best role model.

She throws me an apologetic look. "It's just easier this way. He can stay in his normal routine. I already made arrangements with Justin's mom." She turns her gaze back to Geo. "She'll pick you and Justin up from school."

"But–" Geo starts to protest.

"It'll be okay," I say. Because my job is to make Julia's life easier, not more complicated. "You stay with your friend. If you need anything, I'm only a phone call away."

The relief that passes over Julia's face shouldn't cut so deep.

Fuck.

I may have earned her forgiveness, but I haven't proven myself worthy.

It's quite possible I never will.

* * *

Julia

Channing does the dishes with Geo then finds me finishing some last minute emails in my office.

"I'm almost done fixing your car–I can have it done by the time you get back from your trip. I can give you a ride to the airport," he tells me.

"No need. My boss is sending a car. We're taking his jet."

His brows arch. "Well, hoity toity Mr. Burns."

I give him a look that says *Stop*.

"I don't like him."

"That's interesting. He doesn't like you."

He leans against the door, not ruffled at all. "You're mad at me."

"I'm not mad, I just–"

"Is it because I taught Geo to drive? Or the hot wiring the car thing? Or because I told him about my missions?" He gives me that *aw, shucks* expression, which makes it impossible to stay annoyed.

Still, someone needs to draw boundaries here because Channing clearly doesn't know what's appropriate with Geo and what's not.

"All of the above. Do me a favor–skip the lessons on criminal activities and focus on helping him with his wolf? Leave the normal parenting to me."

His expression doesn't change, and yet I fear I've hurt him. "You got it, babe." He reaches for me, pulling me into the circle of his arms. He seems to have brushed off my harsh words about parenting, but I feel guilty. Especially when I know Channing struggles with feeling like a fuck-up.

But Geo's my kid. *Mi vida*. Everything to me. I know I'm probably over-protective, but I have to be. I'm a single parent. I didn't have a village or a pack to help me raise this kid.

I have family, but they're in Nogales, on the Mexican side of the border. We don't get to see them as often as I wish.

"Let me make it up to you?" Channing crooks that panty-melting smile of his, and I feel even guiltier.

His hands slide down and mold around my ass. I loop my arms around his neck and jump to straddle him, knowing my

Alpha's Command

weight won't knock him over. He makes me feel young again. Limber. Sexy.

He carries me into the bedroom, his beautiful muscles bulging and rippling as he lays me down in the center of the bed. I don't lie back and let him do this thing, though. I'm the aggressor this time. Maybe I want to make up for the fact that I don't trust him. Or that I probably hurt him.

I rise up on my knees and tear his shirt off, then reach for the button on his jeans. He kicks off his boots, his breath quickening.

It amazes me that this young, virile man finds me so attractive. That he still wants me, even after I offended him. I get his zipper open and fist his cock, dragging the skin down toward the tip, reveling in the way it surges and lengthens even more in my hand.

Channing kicks his jeans and boxer briefs off then pulls off my blouse and works off my bra.

I urge him up on the bed and onto his back, so I can crawl over his legs and take his length into my mouth.

"Oh, Fates," he croaks the moment my tongue hits the head of his cock. I take him into the pocket of my cheek a few times, then pop off and lick around the head. "Jewels."

I take him into my mouth again and hum in response, fisting the base of his cock and sliding my hand up and down in concert with my mouth, so it feels like I'm taking him all the way in.

He grips my head, fingers gripping my hair roughly then releasing and massaging my scalp, like he just remembered to be gentle.

I love it.

Love getting this response from him. Giving something back. Making him feel good the way he's pleasured me.

I massage his balls with one hand and suck hard, hollowing my cheeks.

Channing's breath grows raspy and ragged. He slaps the bed beside his leg. "Climb on me, Jewels," he pants. "I want you to come with me."

I slow down, licking his balls, tracing the vein on the underside of his cock. Then I scoot off the bed to tug off my yoga pants.

Channing grabs a condom from the bedside table and rolls it on. He's up on his knees again, but I push on his chest, forcing–ha, as if that were possible–him onto his back.

He complies, green eyes gleaming in the darkness.

I climb over him and lower myself onto his erection, not needing any more foreplay than the blowjob. His arousal works to arouse me. My internal muscles clench in satisfaction, and Channing growls, reaching for my hips to tug me down. To take him deeper.

"Oh God." My hands drop to his broad shoulders, and I rock my hips over his, grinding my clit against his loins.

His fingers tighten on my hips, and he helps me, urging me forward and back, finding a sustainable rhythm. "That's it, Jewels. Take me deep. Chase your pleasure."

I toss my head back. Bare my teeth. Imagine I'm a she-wolf taking what she wants. I don't know why that helps me feel unbound, but it does. Like I can let my animal side free. Not that I have an animal side. Not like Channing.

I work my hips over Channing's, growing slicker every moment. Growing more wild. More free.

And then, it's not enough.

Channing seems to know the moment I need a change because he flips our bodies in a deft roll, bringing his above mine. In this position, he slams into me, gripping the headboard so hard it cracks, and he has to shift his hand to push back against the wall.

And then we come. I climax. He follows. The room spins. Fills with rainbows. Gold glitterdust. Shooting stars.

He slows the rhythm, but keeps rocking until he's wrung every last drop of pleasure from me. Even after he's rolled us to our sides, he eases in and out of me, sending more aftershocks through me.

His kiss on my forehead is tender. Like I mean something to him.

"I'm sorry about the thing with Geo," I murmur in the darkness, after he's disposed of the condom, and I'm snuggled up against his chest.

"It's all good," he says, automatically.

For some reason, though, I'm still certain it's not.

Chapter Eleven

Julia

On the morning of my business trip, I arrive at the small landing strip in my best silk blouse and skirt suit set, relaxed from an early-morning ride on Channing's tongue. This is my first time on a private jet, but I can't summon the excitement. I wish I were back home with Geo. And Channing.

It's only been a couple of weeks, but I can't imagine the house without his presence.

"This way, ma'am," the chauffeur guides me, taking my small bag.

I blow out a breath and put my game face on. I'm here to work.

Inside the jet is as luxurious as I imagined.

"Julia, welcome aboard." Mr. van den Berg lounges on a couch, a glass of scotch in his hand. He waves for me to settle in, and I sink into one of the white leather seats.

"And how is young Geo?"

I try, but I can't seem to smile. "Eating me out of house and home," I report because I know it'll make him laugh.

He chuckles. "I appreciate you suggesting this face-to-face meeting. I hope Geo will be able to manage without you."

"Of course."

"He's not old enough to leave home alone, now?"

I hesitate. *I don't trust him,* Channing's warning flashes in my head. Wolves are by nature protective, but they also have good instincts. I remember that about Geoffrey. If he had a bad feeling about someone, it was usually right.

But this is my boss, and he's just being polite, asking about my kid. It's small talk. I push away the unease. "Oh no, he's staying with a friend."

The flight attendant offers me champagne, and I accept. I pretend to sip the liquid while anxiety bubbles in my stomach.

"So your brother-in-law is gone?"

I'm sure his questions are just friendly, and I normally enjoy the interest he takes in my personal life, but for some reason, today it feels intrusive. So, I answer vaguely, "He's in and out. He has a flexible job."

Mr. van den Berg sips his drink and nods.

To cut off any further questions, I pull out my laptop and open it up to the contract to review.

* * *

Channing

Geo's with his friend. Julia's gone. I could go for a run,

but my wolf doesn't feel like it. He'd rather hang around the house and wallow in her scent. The house is too quiet without her and Geo.

I better get used to it. Geo's wolf is almost settled. Any day now, I'm bound to do something stupid, and Julia's going to kick me out. I don't know what I'll do then. Go back to my pack? Keep going on missions? That worked for a decade, but not anymore. It'll take an act of Fate to keep me away from Julia a second time.

Around nine pm, I get a text. *Fight club tonight. You coming?*

The number isn't saved, but I know it's probably Trey or Jared on a burner.

Can't tonight, I text back. *Babysitting.*

Babysitting? The texter replies. It's probably Trey because we give each other shit all the time. *Did one of your baby mamas finally hunt you down?*

Yeah, that's Trey.

I grin—not because my reputation as a player is firmly intact—but because my wolf likes the idea of Julia as my baby mama. Maybe I can goad someone to call Julia my baby mama to her face. She'd kill them where they stood.

Something like that.

They have to be desperate to ask you to help.

The smile slides from my face, and I pocket my phone. I know it's a joke, but jokes are only funny because of the grain of truth behind them. Even my friends know I'm not to be trusted with a kid.

I head outside to work on Julia's car. I need one more part to fix the transmission, but I can wrap up the rest with the portable floodlight. Buddy borrowed my truck and left his car parked on the other side of the cul-de-sac. He'll be back with pizza and the part.

A few hours later, my phone buzzes with another text. I almost ignore it because I suspect it's Trey ragging on me. My wolf is restless tonight, unable to settle.

Instinct makes me glance at the text. It's from Geo. *Can you pick me up?*

A cold feeling spreads over me. I call him, and he answers on the first ring.

"Hey," his voice is low, like he's keeping the call a secret.

"What's wrong?" I ask. All the things that could be going wrong flash through my head. Geo's wolf on a rampage, outing itself to the family. Geo hurt. Geo accidentally hurting someone else.

"I don't know," Geo hesitates.

"Are you riled up?" By *you*, I mean his wolf. "Did you forget to do your homework?" *I need to do my homework* means his wolf is restless and wants to get away from people, maybe to shift.

"I forgot my medication," he repeats the code I taught him that means his wolf wants extraction asap.

"I got you, Geo. I'll be there ASAP." I'm already striding down the driveway. "Text me the address."

"Thanks. What do I tell Mrs. Meyers?"

I check my phone. It's eleven pm. "I can explain to her and your mom. Sneak out of the house now."

"Okay. I think I'm okay."

"Better safe than sorry. Trust your instincts. Do me a

favor and call your mom? Let her know you forgot your medication. She knows the code."

"Thanks, Uncle Channing."

"Not a problem. You did good, Geo. Call me back if you need."

My steps slow as I approach my bike. I loaned Buddy the truck, and Julia's car has parts missing. I could take Buddy's car, but he didn't leave the keys, so I'd have to hotwire it. Even then, he never has much gas in the tank, and the engine is unreliable at best. Do I take the time and risk Geo and me coming home smelling like pot?

I better take my bike. It's not like I'm in the running for a parent of the year award. When Julia finds out, she'll shoot me. She'll have to craft a special bullet to do any damage, but that won't stop her. She'll melt down the silverware herself.

It won't matter. I need to get Geo out of a tense situation.

Maybe that's why my wolf has been riled up all evening. It knew that something was wrong.

Maybe my instincts are on point after all.

* * *

I pull up to Geo"s friend's house and grab my phone. I try a few times to dial Julia, but it goes immediately to voice message.

Geo slinks from the shadows alongside the house carrying his backpack. Whatever instinct told me something was wrong dies at the sight of him. He looks calm and relaxed, not fighting the wolf at all. Maybe he just wanted to hang with me.

The thought sets off a starburst of warmth in my chest.

"Mom's going to shit a brick," he announces, grinning as I hand him the helmet.

I smile back at him. "Extenuating circumstances. Always ask forgiveness not permission. You hungry?"

His stomach growls loud enough to echo through the neighborhood. Maybe that's why he couldn't sleep.

"Hop on before the neighbors think we're doing a drug deal," I say, and he does. "We'll stop and get Chinese takeout."

Riding at night is one of my favorite things. The cool air, the endless blackness. It exhilarates me.

It's not how I expected to give Geo his first motorcycle ride, but this was an emergency, so why not enjoy it?

Geo hugs me and leans into the curves like a pro. I should teach him to ride the bike on his own. He's big enough to handle it. Old enough to understand safety measures. Not legally, but who cares about that?

I'm almost to the restaurant when I notice the black SUV turning onto the street behind us. It would be nothing, except that there's another black SUV identical to it up ahead, one that's been with us since we came out of the neighborhood.

I stop at the light and instead of taking the turn to the restaurant, bang a U-ey and reverse course.

"Hey," Geo bawls in my ear. "That was the restaurant."

"Change of plans," I tell him. The SUV following us makes the same U-turn. My instincts were right. "We're being followed."

Geo squeezes my middle.

The black SUV knows it's been made. It zooms close, not

bothering to hide the fact that it's tailing us. Up close, it's obvious it's been altered. Why would someone be driving an armored car down the sleepy streets of Flagstaff, Arizona?

I've got a bad feeling about this. Really bad.

"Hold tight," I tell Geo, even though he already is. I rev the bike into a higher gear, taking an illegal turn. If a cop sees me and lights up, it'll be the least of my problems. A cop might help us at this point. I can leave Geo with them and zoom off to face these guys on my own turf.

Another black SUV darts out and joins the first two. Who are these guys? They're well funded, if they can afford this many armored cars.

As I zip down side streets and through red lights, trying to lose them, I rack my brain for who would target me like this. All the missions I've done, all the blood I've spilled, the enemies I've taken out—I can't think of one who'd track me down like this.

It doesn't matter. All that matters is getting Geo out alive.

"I'm trying to lose these guys," I tell him. "Just hang tight."

"Got it." There's a little growl in his voice. His wolf understands we're in danger.

"If I crash or we get stopped, I need you to turn into a wolf," I shout against the wind, "and run as fast and far as you can, deep into the wilderness. Your wolf will know what to do. Promise me, Geo."

"What about you?" he asks.

"I'll be fine. As soon as I can, I'll radio for help."

My maneuvers get me through town unaccompanied. I speed down the empty road, watching for a tail. I'm about to declare us home free when another black SUV appears ahead. It crosses the road and stops straddling the yellow line, trying to drive me back to his buddy's waiting arms. As if I'd be that stupid.

I make it look like I'm going to turn around, and at the last minute zip off to the side, gunning down the breakdown lane. We pass the stopped SUV with a spray of gravel.

I continue down the road, but I don't fool myself that I've lost them. They've got eyes in the sky or something tracking me. If Geo wasn't clinging to me, I'd look around for a drone.

What now? I don't dare lead them home. I'd have more options if I were alone. I'd be more reckless, for one thing. Every cell in my body is focused on the smaller body barnacled to my back.

I need backup.

I wait until we're on a straight stretch of road and pull out my phone. I hit the emergency call button, the one that lights up our command center with an SOS. I can't rely too much on my pack. They're miles away in Taos.

But I do have some friends in the area. Tonight they're all gathered in one place.

Julia will kill me when she finds out where we've been. But she will find out because we'll have made it home alive.

I take the next turn, setting a course for the abandoned commercial strip where Trey and Jared, and a bunch of fight-hungry shifters will be waiting.

* * *

Julia

Alpha's Command

The tightness in my chest eases a little when my ride pulls up to my small house.

I hop out, waving off the driver's help to get my small bag. "Thank you," I call and hike up the driveway.

I don't know why I felt the need to come home early. Every motherly instinct I had was blaring an alert. I felt stupid when I booked the last minute flight from New York– I didn't even text Geo. He'd be asleep at his friend's house, and I didn't want him to worry.

I took a ride share from the airport. My phone died while it was on airplane mode and in my rush to pack, I left the charger at the hotel. Everything in me told me I had to get home.

Now I'm here, and things don't feel right.

The windows are dark and quiet, but the floodlight Channing uses to work at night is on, pointed towards my car. Pieces and parts of socket wrenches are scattered around it. It's not like him to leave his tools out. Or is it? I guess I don't know him all that well.

I plug my phone in. It blares to life, and I scramble to check my messages. I missed several calls from Channing and Geo.

I hit redial. Nothing. My return calls to both of them go to voicemail.

It's past midnight. Where could they be? Channing's truck is here. But his bike is gone.

I'm going to kill him. As soon as I figure out where Geo is.

I take a second to listen to Geo's voice message. *I forgot my medicine*–the code Channing taught us to use when we're around humans. Guilt stabs me. I should've let Geo stay home with Channing.

A horrible sputtering noise outside brings me to the door. Buddy pulls up to the curb in his old Charger.

"Buddy," I cry. "Where's Channing? Did he get Geo?"

He blinks at me. "I just got back. I haven't seen them."

A chill runs through me. It's been over an hour since Geo left the message. They should be back by now. Maybe they shifted to run from Justin's neighborhood? Like, an emergency shift?

I wrap my arms around myself with a shiver. My instincts are screaming at me. Something's wrong.

Before I panic completely, I remember Geo has a tracking app I installed on his phone. I can see him, and he can see me.

"Stay here," I order Buddy and run back inside to stab at my phone screen and find the map with the blinking light that tells me where Geo is. He's not at his friend's Justin's house nor anywhere nearby. No, it looks like he's on the outskirts of Flagstaff, an area I'm not too familiar with. There's nothing on that side of town but some warehouses. I have no idea where Channing is taking my son, but I can guess.

"I'm going to kill him," I growl and grab my phone. I march out and head down the driveway to the curb, where I wrench open Buddy's passenger door. A bunch of soda cans and fast food wrappers fall out, and I sweep the rest to the car floor so there's room for me to sit. "Take me here," I order, pointing to the map on my phone. "Now."

* * *

Channing

The wind whips my face as I lean into a turn. Behind me, Geo leans too. My phone's been vibrating nonstop in my pocket. At the first available moment, I ease it out and hold it to my mouth.

"Little busy," I shout.

"Looks like you're heading to the pop up club." Lance's voice is cool. He's been manning the coms more and more since he knocked up his mate. I can imagine him there now, holding the tiny bundle of his daughter, walking her when she's fussy. For once, the thought doesn't bring despair. Lance made a family work for him. Maybe there's hope for me.

Weird that I'm thinking about that sort of thing in the middle of a high speed chase, but my brain does that sometimes.

"Yeah, gonna visit Jared and Trey. But I've got company." The three SUVs on my tail are still there. They're slower than I am, but they seem to know where my bike will end up before I do.

"10/4. Deke's on his way, but he's six hours out. I've alerted Jared and Trey that you're coming in hot with uninvited guests. They're expecting you."

"Good. These fuckers need a welcoming committee."

"How many?"

"Three in cages. Maybe more. They're everywhere." A fourth SUV darts out of a side road to join the others, and I break off with a string of curses. "Make that four."

"Hang tight. Get to the fight club. I'm monitoring your position."

I shove my phone away without hanging up. I put on a burst of speed, gunning to outrun them. I've been careful because of Geo and the fear of running out of gas, but no more.

"We're almost there," I tell Geo. "You've done great."

He hugs me tighter. Kid's got a death grip on my middle. If I were human, I'd have bruises on my ribs. "Who are these guys?"

"Wish I knew. Soon it won't matter." Once I get Geo to safety, my plan is to wipe these guys from the face of the earth. They tried to fuck with me, and it impacted my family.

We're almost to the turn off into the commercial strip where Jared's hosting the fight club when a roar cuts the air.

A dozen Harleys have joined the chase.

I risk a look back. The head Harley holds a familiar face. *Hannibal*.

These aren't definitely not friendlies, then. Now this mess makes more sense. Hannibal's got it out for me. What I don't know is where he got the funding for the army of SUVs and motorcycles. Maybe he has a rich backer?

I'll think about later. The SUVs couldn't keep up with my crotch rocket, but Hannibal can. I increase my speed past where I feel comfortable. With Geo on the bike, I'm being less reckless.

I can't let Hannibal and his hog buddies get ahead of me. They'll stop to cut me off, and it'll be game over. I can't fight them all.

But my friends at fight club can.

I cut between the warehouses, heading towards my final destination. Hannibal's bike rips the air behind me.

Because Lance told me Jared and Trey would prepare a welcoming committee, I see a booby trap ahead of me. Moonlight glints on the wire stretched across the road. The shadows obscure most of the trap—and the ramp someone placed to the side for me.

"Hang on," I holler to Geo. This poor kid's going to need therapy after this.

Hannibal's so close, I can smell his clove cologne. I rush towards the wire, swerving right at the last second. We hit the ramp and go airborne.

We fly over the wire. Ahead of us is a long, dark stretch of road lined with warehouses, and the fight club warehouse at the far end, closest to the forest. Fires flicker against the tree line. Looks like Trey and Jared prepared a welcome party, fireworks and all.

I just have to make it that far. My bike crashes down, wheels first, thank Fate, and I speed away, Geo's startled laugh echoing in my ears.

Maybe he'll be okay. Maybe I'll save the day and make everyone proud. Julia will forgive me, and we can be a family. Lance and Deke figured out the mate thing. How hard can it be?

Behind us, the razor wire did its thing stopping the calvary. It won't stop all of them, though. Those armored cars will smash right through it.

A bike revs to my left and right. Looks like a few Harley's skidded under the wire. They're gaining on us—until several dark shapes blur from the shadows, cackling. The werehyenas swing lead pipes, smashing them into the chests of the bikers. The Harleys go down, and I'm free to speed into the parking lot, weaving between bonfires.

I stop in front of the warehouse as Trey and Jared step out. They're barefoot and shirtless. Ready to shift.

"That was so awesome," Geo whoops as he tumbles to the pavement.

"You okay?" I ask, adrenaline still rushing in my ears.

He gives me a thumbs up. Kid's gonna be fine.

"The razor wire was a nice touch," I say. "How'd you know there'd be bikes?"

"We've got eyes in the air," Jared points to the sky. "They clocked the bikes chasing you and relayed it to us in time. The cheetahs strung the wire with seconds to spare."

"Who'd you bring us, brother?" Trey asks.

"A dozen hogs carrying shifters of some kind. I don't know." I talk fast. In the distance, a werehyena screeches. "Their leader, Hannibal's got a beef with me. He challenged me at the last fight club. I don't know his animal. Plus there are four or more SUVs–armored vehicles of some kind." Engines rev, just out of sight.

"Got it." Trey nods to Jared, who steps off and signals a group of werecheetahs hanging at the end of the parking lot. "Thanks for the rundown. But I meant the kid."

"Oh, him?" I drop a hand on Geo's shoulder. "This is my nephew, Geo."

A werehyena comes running out of the darkness. "They're coming."

The werecheetahs rev their bikes and take off towards

the fray. No sign of Hannibal, yet. I bet that fucker survived the wire.

"The big guy, Hannibal," I say to Trey and Jared, who's returned. "He's mine."

They nod. "We'll take care of the rest. We've got backup."

More shadows detach from the side of the warehouse and step into the light. Two big guys and three more smaller ones lurking behind. Shifters, all of them. Here for the fight club.

"We're ready," says the biggest guy. I think I recognize him. I squint at his scarred face, searching for a memory of his name.

I do recognize the shifter standing beside him. Caleb, pulling on his beard, a thoughtful expression on his face.

"Oh hey, man." I step in to shake his hand. "You joining the party?"

"Came here to fight. Might as well get one." Like Trey and Jared, he's barefoot. "Have you met Grizz?"

I swallow my *holy shit*. Caleb and Grizz are legends. The only one more famous is Nash. If shifters had action figures, the three of them would be the collector's set.

"I thought you were retired?" I say to Grizz. He's a big, mean-looking bastard with a fucked up face. I don't know who in the hell he fought to get scarred up like that, and I don't want to know.

He shrugs.

Howls ring out, interspersed with the *rat tat tat* of a machine gun. The werecheetahs found the enemy. Good thing we're in the middle of nowhere, or we'd have police and firemen on the scene.

"Guys." Trey nudges me. "We're about to get company."

"Right. Geo." I tighten my grip on his shoulder "A big fight's gonna go down. We're making a stand. But you need to be out of sight."

His eyes are huge and shifter bright. "I want to help."

"I know. I need you to stay alive and stay safe, so you can protect your mom if something happens to me. Will you accept your mission?"

He nods, so sober I get a glimpse of how he'll look as an adult. Like my brother.

"And what will you do?"

"I'm gonna fight." Normally I would grin and say something like, "I'm going to have some fun" but with Geo here, the danger feels real. I need to be serious. More like an alpha. Take care of the pup under my protection.

"C'mon," one of the smaller shifters says. A dark haired Irishman–one of the bookies. "This way." His two other bookie friends–the grey haired one and the one who sneezes feathers–are already at the tree line.

"Go with them." I give Geo a gentle push. "You need to stay out of sight and be ready to shift and run in case the tide of battle turns. It won't, but it's good to have a backup plan. Listen to these guys," I nod to the three bookies. "and do what they say."

I wait until Geo's almost to the forest before joining my friends.

"My priority is Geo's safety," I tell them.

"Noted," Jared says. "If anything happens, Laurie will airlift him out."

I'm guessing Laurie is the one with the feathers.

"Nothing will touch him," Grizz rumbles. I don't know him from another shifter, but I believe him. He'd fight and give his life for my nephew. In this moment, we are pack.

As one, Grizz, Caleb and I strip off our leather jackets and toss them against the warehouse. Shirts and shoes are next. Our bare feet crunch over broken glass as we rejoin Jared and Trey, walking towards the other edge of parking lot. We pass a small bonfire, and Jared leans in and lights a long match. He carries it a few feet and touches it to the ground where it smells like someone's poured a line of gasoline. Flames shoot up and race ahead to light our way.

Trey whoops. "Let's get this party started!"

Caleb and Grizz are silent, focused. I take my place beside them. Normally I'd be yodeling a war cry with Trey, but tonight the stakes are higher than they've ever been.

A cheetah comes hurtling from the road, on his bike, chased by three Harleys. He leads them on a winding route around the fires, but they're coming straight for us. The welcoming committee.

The Harleys are almost on us.

"Left," Caleb calls.

"I'll take right," Trey offers. He and Jared step to the side.

"I got center." Grizz cracks his knuckles, and it sounds like gunshots.

The werecheetah zips past us. The Harleys are so close, we can see the whites of the rider's eyes. Their eyes are glowing–they're shifters, every last one of them.

At the last second, Trey and Jared dart forward. Trey leaps and kicks the rider off the bike to Jared, who finishes him off.

Caleb lunges to the side and grabs his opponent, plucking him off the Harley and tossing him to the ground. There's a crunch, and I turn away before I watch the enemy rider's fate.

Grizz doesn't move. He waits until the Harley's on top of him, then grabs the handlebars and lets out a roar. In an unbelievable show of strength, he lifts the entire heavy motorcycle over his head and smashes the entire hog to the ground.

The rider goes bouncing over the pavement and comes to rest close to me. I skip a foot and kick the downed rider in the head, hard enough to snap his neck.

Three seconds, and it's over. We took the first line out without bothering to shift. The ultimate insult.

Trey rises from the body he's searching, holding a weapon–a big bore revolver. "They have silver bullets." His eyes glow the color of liquid mercury.

"They're shifters." Jared sniffs, gets a nose full of clove cologne and coughs. "I don't know what type."

"They're here to kill someone." Caleb examines the gun he took off his downed opponent. "The only reason to carry a silver bullet is to shoot a shifter dead."

Everyone looks at me.

"Sorry, guys. Don't know what I did to piss them off."

"Doesn't matter how it started," Grizz's normal growly voice is swallowed up by the rumble of his bear. "We're going to end it. Tonight."

I make a mental note to never get on Grizz's bad side. Just the sound of his bear's roar is enough to stop a lesser man's heart.

An explosion booms. The source is out of sight, but it was big enough to shake the ground. Eerie laughter echoes all around.

"Did the hyenas bring big guns?" I ask Trey.

"No," he says, as serious as I've ever seen him. "I think that was your friends."

"They're not my friends," I say. "After tonight, they're off my Christmas card list."

That gets a snicker.

An SUV barrels from the road, chased by cheetah bikes. One of the cheetahs zips in front of it and wrecks, sacrificing his bike to stop the SUV. The cheetah rolls to safety but the armored vehicle rolls over the bike and keeps coming.

A familiar whistle of a launched rocket makes the hair on the back of my neck rise.

"Incoming," Caleb shouts, and we scatter. The rocket whines as it shoots past us and hits the warehouse. *Boom!*

"Get clear," I shout as debris rains down. The front of the warehouse collapses, its steel frame creaking.

Geo's startled cry reaches my ears. "Stay back," I shout, waving an arm. He's at the forest line, standing frozen. "Get him out of here." I point to the bookies, who are trying to drag Geo back.

"Airlift," the Irishman shouts.

The grey headed shifter puts his fingers to his lips and lets out a piercing whistle.

A giant owl swoops down from the trees and grasps Geo's

arms, lifting him into the air. Its huge wings flap as he carries Geo off. He'll be safe, deep in the woods.

Metal crunches. A huge bear has attacked the armed SUV, scoring the sides with its giant claws.

Trey and Jared rip off the doors and drag out the driver and passengers. Bullets crack and bodies slump to the ground. Since the enemy brought the silver bullets, it'd be a shame to waste them.

More dark shapes pour out of the road on foot. No sign of Hannibal in the smoky air.

Grizz is still in human form, marching into the fray. I catch up with him, and we both start to run.

There's a drum beat in my head, a soundtrack for war. Cheetahs zoom in and out, their bikes buzzing like angry hornets. Two more SUVs cut through the smoke, ramming through the line of cheetah bikes.

Grizz and I separate. I get a running start and leap on top of one SUV, scoring the roof with my claws. The metal squeals, opening the top like a tin can to pluck out the enemy within.

Bullets blast into my face. One of them nicks me, and the silver burns. I relax and let my wolf come.

The passenger rises up, aiming a gun, and gets a face full of claw. I lunge forward as a wolf and close my jaws over his head. *Crunch.*

The driver stands in his seat, aiming for me. I look down the barrel and see my death.

A flash of white descends. The huge owl clamps its claws on the driver's shoulders and lifts him up. The owl flaps its wings, gaining height with the struggling enemy in its claws.

The driver cries out, spraying bullets wildly. Before he can aim, the owl shrieks and lets go.

The enemy crashes to earth, where a swipe of Caleb's bear claw puts an end to him.

I release my kill and lope down the windshield, back into the fight.

The SUV Grizz took out is upside down, wheels spinning in the air. A huge bear lumbers away, its fur spattered with gasoline and blood. Its size takes my breath away. Legend says that Grizz's bear has thick brown fur like a Kodiak bear on steroids. One who can bench press a Mac truck. It rises to its hind feet and roars. All around me, cheetahs yip and hyenas cackle.

Smoke stings my wolf eyes.

A shape takes form in the gray smog. A giant in a leather jacket. Hannibal, his face contorted. His clothing is starting to rip as his animal fights to the surface. He sees me and roars. "Rematch!"

I snarl and race towards him.

He pulls out a gun and shoots. I dodge and keep running. Bullets skim my fur. I put on a burst of speed and leap, my fangs aiming for his throat.

He bursts out of his clothes, his form morphing into a massive monster. He's huge and muscular, with two giant horns. I hit his chest and knock him back a step. My fangs score at his shoulder, but his skin is thick, and I can't get purchase. I twist and bound away.

Goading him to shift has its benefits. He dropped his gun and let it skid to the side. Without the threat of silver bullets, I'm free to rip and tear into him.

He's wicked strong and fast, but not as fast as I am. I dart in and out, snapping at his limbs. He bellows and tries to stomp my wolf, but I weave through his legs, slicing at the insides of his knees. First blood.

I'm too slow getting away, and his arms clamp around me. I twist, my fangs seeking his throat. He clamps his arms around me. My bones crack as he squeezes.

I shift back to man form. Suddenly I'm a lot smaller than the animal he was holding, and he staggers. I fall to my back, dragging him with me, and kick out my legs, launching him over my head. He crashes to the pavement ten feet behind me.

Three cheetah shifters leap on him. A second later, they're flying through the air.

Damn, how am I gonna beat this guy?

A rocket whistles by and an SUV explodes. Flaming chunks of twisted metal rain down.

I lose sight of Hannibal in the thick smoke. My ears ring. I can barely hear the crack of gun fire followed by a pained bellow.

To my left, the enemy is making a last stand. Grizz's giant bear wades into their ranks. His claws are so big, one swipe sends their heads rolling. Their bodies crumple. Beheading is the easiest way to bring down a shifter. Grizz elevates the grisly task to an art form.

I give him a thumbs up, and he displays teeth the size of my forearm and lets out a roar that I'm pretty sure means, "Great work, bestie!"

Hannibal's gun lies on the pavement. I scoop it up and go

Alpha's Command

hunting. I follow the trail of werecheetah bodies until I find him. His telltale horns emerge from the smoke.

"Hannibal," I shout. I'm limping–must have caught a bullet. The wound burns the way silver does.

I rack the shotgun, but it's out of bullets. I toss it between us. There. Now we face each other, animal to animal.

He stomps the pavement like a bull. My wolf is ready to take over when there's a whooshing sound behind me.

A group of werehyenas have taken control of the final SUV. They've pulled up close and are aiming the launcher at Hannibal....and me.

"No, wait!" I holler. Too late. One of the hyenas shrieks and launches the weapon.

I drop and eat gravel. The rocket whistles overhead, the zooming sound blending with Hannibal's roars.

The boom deafens me. I leap to my feet as soon as I can, but there's no sign of Hannibal. Just a crater and a ring of soot in the place where he stood.

I curse.

Other than the crackling bonfires and the distant screech of a hyena, the parking lot is quiet. The fight is over.

Trey and Jared have shifted back to human form. Their bodies are stained red. They're not limping, so I assume most of the blood isn't theirs.

"Hannibal?" I ask. "Big guy with horns?"

Trey shakes his head. "He took off."

"What the hell is he," Jared mutters. "A fucking minotaur?"

"I don't know. But this isn't over."

A shout makes me turn. Geo comes running. "That was

so cool. When you turned into a wolf and leaped on that car—"

"You liked that?" It's on the tip of my tongue to tell him *wait until you see me fight another wolf* but a sound across the way makes my hair stand up.

An old Charger putters into sight, rolling around the smoking piles of debris. Jared's head snaps around.

"They're friendlies," I shout to forestall any defensive violence.

Why is Buddy here?

Someone shrieks, and the passenger door opens. Julia races out, her face pale.

Aww, crap.

"Geoffrey," she cries. Tears make her voice wobble.

"Mom!" Geo sounds like he's enjoyed a day riding roller coasters at an amusement park. Julia chokes back a sob and throws her arms around him. "It's okay, mom. I'm all right."

Buddy gets out of the driver's seat and shuffles to my side. "Sorry. She has a tracker on Geo's phone. I couldn't stop her, so I figured it was better to come with."

I wave off the apology. It wasn't like I was going to hide the truth from Julia. But to have her see the aftermath of my dangerous life this way isn't great.

"I'm okay," Geo keeps telling her. "We're okay."

But I see the parking lot through Julia's eyes. Bonfires burning against the backdrop of a collapsed warehouse. Bodies of shifters—friendlies and enemies alike—littering the scorched pavement. A pack of werehyenas joyriding past in the stolen SUV, waving weapons and whooping. And her

Alpha's Command

precious son in the middle of the chaos. I did all this to keep him safe, but it looks bad.

Time to face the music.

Geo's had enough of Julia's fussing. He pulls away and hollers to me. "Hey, Uncle Channing, did you get shot?"

"Shot?" Julia gasps.

"Yeah, Mom, they had silver bullets. They were after Uncle Channing."

She glances at me but doesn't meet my eyes. Her face is a mask of fear and fury. "What happened?"

"These cars started following us." Geo points to the bombed out SUVs, and Julia's eye bug out. "A bunch of them. Uncle Channing had me on the bike and started doing evasive maneuvers."

"I had the truck," Buddy offers. "That's why Channing took the bike." It's kind of him to defend me, but it's not going to be enough to convince Julia that I'm not completely irresponsible.

"And then we came here and *boom*! They blew the warehouse..." Geo continues a graphic play-by-play of the battle, complete with sound effects. Digging my grave deeper and deeper.

Not that I don't deserve it.

Julia's gaze travels from the collapsed building to her son's face to the scorch marks on the pavement. Geo runs out of steam, and she looks in my direction.

"Is this true?" she asks me.

"Yeah," I say. "That about sums it up." No use defending myself. In some ways, it's a relief to let the blame rest on me.

"Get in the car," she tells Geo, her voice shaking.

"But–" Geo protests.

Two werecheetahs rush by, carrying a can of gasoline. They toss it onto the nearest bonfire and howl with the flames shoot into the sky.

"Listen to your mother," I order, and Geo drags his feet but disappears into the backseat of the Charger.

I wait until Julia's settled next to him before approaching. "Julia."

"No," she holds a hand up to forestall my explanation. She's not meeting my eyes.

"Geo's okay. I would never let anything happen to him."

"They were following us, Mom," Geo puts in from the other side of the car. "We had to get away!"

"They tailed us from Justin's house. I don't know how. I radioed for help, but the only place I could bring him was here. At least here, I had backup." I nod towards Trey and Jared, who are standing and chatting with Grizz and Caleb, all four of them buck naked.

She averts her eyes. "Was this you?" she asks in a low voice. "This is your" –she waves a hand in the air– "business?"

I know what she means. I kept Geo alive, but the reason he was in danger was me.

It's my fault. I'll own it. "Yes."

She nods, still not looking at me.

"Take them home," I tell Buddy. "I'll be right along."

From the look on Julia's face, I'm no longer welcome there. But I'll stand guard on the porch tonight. My wolf won't allow anything less.

Come morning, though, I'll be gone. I'll leave Buddy and

the cameras watching over Geo and Julia. It'll be better for them if I leave, go far away. I brought danger to their doorstep, and I'll never forgive myself for that.

"Why so serious?" One of the werehyenas laughs in my face. "We won!" His buddies cheer.

A wolfish whine catches in my throat as I watch the Charger roll away.

I won the battle and lost the war.

***

Julia

I shake and sweat the entire way home. This is too much. I can't take it. Driving up on that scene ground in the fact that Channing doesn't belong here with us.

He's in a high-risk job.

He loves danger. He always has. So do his friends.

And I care too much about him to be able to stomach his profession. Not only that, but there's no way in hell I'm letting him infect Geo with his wild and reckless lifestyle.

No way in hell.

That boy is all I have. He's my entire world. And to think that Channing dragged him into whatever the hell that was breaks my heart.

It kills me that he wouldn't know better.

Wouldn't have more consideration. Wouldn't stop and think about whether bringing a *thirteen-year-old boy* into that kind of mayhem would be a good idea.

I mean, I understand he got caught when Geo was with him.

But that means trouble follows him.

And I can't let it follow him to us.

I just can't.

No matter how much I love the guy.

No matter how much I wanted him to stay.

It's time for Channing to go.

I'm not going to stay home while my partner is on missions, holding my breath and dreading the knock on the door from someone telling me he didn't make it.

I did that once.

I can't do it again.

* * *

Channing

When I get to the house, Julia's waiting on the porch. She's thrown a bathrobe over her regular clothes. Her hair holds the faint reek of smoke.

I'll never forgive myself for tonight.

I put a booted foot on the stair, but don't get any closer. Her expression is so lost and tired, I want to hold her. But that's not what she wants right now.

"I don't know how to be with you," she says. "When Geoffrey went on tour, I thought because he was a shifter, he would be impervious to danger. When they came to notify me, I thought they were wrong. Geoffrey was invincible. He couldn't be dead." Her voice catches. With bare feet and her make up scrubbed off, she looks young and vulnerable. As fragile as she was the day of the funeral. "We buried an empty coffin. I kept thinking he'd come back." She rubs her eyes, but they're dry. Like she's all cried out.

I sit on the step, keeping a foot of distance between us.

"I can't do this again," she whispers. I know what she means. *I can't be with you.*

"I know." I stare into the night, my wolf howling inside. He's trapped in a cage of my own making. I don't let him crack my facade.

I have to be strong, for her. "Julia... I'm sorry."

"Thanks for helping Geo. I'll never forget all you've done." She rises and goes inside, shutting the door.

And just like that, it's over.

I sit on the stoop, frozen. I stay like that until the night is over and the first light of dawn torches the sky. Buddy stirs in his Charger. I toss the keys to the truck on the front seat. I put the title in Julia's name. She can give it to Geo on his birthday. Or not.

I'll be long gone. I have to be.

Julia's right. Hannibal came after me. Geo was in danger because of me. I couldn't bear it if danger from my job spilled over to destroy him and Jlulia.

It's better that I stay away.

* * *

Julia

I lie in bed, my pillowcase wet with tears, wondering if I've done the right thing. Channing is still here, sitting on the porch, keeping guard. I can sense his presence.

It'd be so easy to call him back inside and lose myself in his scent, his touch.

But when I close my eyes, I see the battlefield of the warehouse parking lot, littered with bodies, and my thirteen-year-old son standing right in the middle of it.

How can Channing keep us safe when his entire life is dangerous? If tonight was any indication, his missions are a thousand times more dangerous than Geoffrey's.

I can't love someone like that again. Someone I might lose. And I can't put my son at risk. If that makes me a coward, so be it. It's better to be alone than suffer a loss like that again.

The clock beside my bed reads three am. I roll over and tangle with something soft. It's Channing's shirt. It smells like Channing, fresh and woodsy. I clutch it to my chest and let the scent soothe me, and finally sleep comes.

In the morning, Channing's gone. I tell Geo he has a mission, and he'll be busy. Geo nods, accepting this.

I'm distracted at work, so much so that Mr. van den Berg mentions it after a meeting.

"Apologies, sir. We ran into a...rough patch at home."

"Is it your brother-in-law?"

"Partly," I admit. "He's gone. He left. For good."

My boss peers at me. "Is everything all right?"

"Oh yes. We're fine." If I say it firmly enough, maybe it'll be true.

"And everything's set for Geo to go to Woodman?" he asks.

"Yes, thank you."

Geo's been moping lately. I encouraged him to go on a

run, but he says his wolf isn't in the mood. A fresh start will be what he needs. I can hold things together, pretend everything's fine, for Geo. I can guide us through our day-to-day routine, pretending there's not a gaping hole in my heart.

* * *

Channing

"What I don't get is why they targeted you," my alpha, Rafe, muses. I'm on the phone debriefing with him and his brother, Lance.

"I don't know." I rub my face. It's been thirty-six hours since the big fight, but my wolf has barely let me sleep. I have Buddy watching Julia's house, but I stay away while checking the security system every hour on the hour. "They had silver bullets, so they knew they were targeting shifters."

"They wanted to kill you," Rafe muses.

"Then why didn't they shoot me off the bike?" I've mulled over this question over and over until I feel insane.

"You're lucky they didn't. You'd be dead. Their hesitation allowed you to get back up," Rafe says.

I don't feel lucky. I feel like death. But I don't say that.

"The round went to you," Lance says. "But this isn't over."

"Agreed." I bet Hannibal is still out there, licking his wounds, biding his time.

"I got intel from both Jared and Trey, who cleaned up the battlefield. Whoever backed this fight had serious cash," Rafe says.

"Yeah, Channing, why'd you have to go and piss off a billionaire?" Lance jokes.

My silence tells him I'm not in a joking mood. There's an awkward pause.

"Hang on, Deke's trying to join," Lance says. The sound of typing comes over the phone.

"I have news," Deke says. He doesn't sound happy.

"Is this about the app?" Rafe asks. "Did Kylie hack it?"

"Not yet. But I did a few general searches, asked around. Looks like some shifter kids have gone missing."

"Runaways?" Lance asks.

"Some of them. But there's reports of a higher than average amount of shifter teens disappearing."

Images flash through my head, too horrible to dwell on. Teens like the bear shifter triplets, lured from their homes and trapped. Some could be hunted to death.

"Were these kids on the app?" Rafe is asking.

"I can't confirm it. I can't link the two yet, but my gut says yeah." Deke's voice is heavy. "My guess is Hannibal's involved."

Someone set this app up, and creeps like Hannibal infiltrated it to prey on shifter teens.

"We have no proof," Lance says.

"We don't need proof," Rafe says. "We find Hannibal. The answers lie with him."

"On it," Deke says. "Kylie can hack any security system around Flagstaff coordinates."

"I'll put the word out," Lance types furiously. "Alert every shifter pack and family we can. And a BOLO for Hannibal."

"I'll search the area where we last saw him," I say. I'm still in Flagstaff. I can't bring myself to leave.

Part of me wants to drive over to Julia's house right now, put her and Geo under house arrest. Because that will get her to forgive me.

I shoot a text to Buddy, asking him to keep eyes on the house. He texts back a picture of the front of Julia's house. With the new door and windows, it looks brand new.

The sight makes me ache.

I shake my head and force myself to focus on Rafe's final orders.

"Watch your six," he says. "You see anything, you radio for backup."

I hang up. My wolf is unsettled. I knew Hannibal was trouble, but this is nuclear. A shifter like him, preying on kids? I'm going to hunt the fucker down and put him in the ground. It's my life's purpose.

After that, I'll ask Rafe to give me a mission on the other side of the world. Something dangerous and lucrative that will take all my focus. Maybe if I spill enough blood, I'll drive the scent of lilac and lavender out of my head.

Chapter Twelve

Julia

Friday comes, and my eyes are bleary from staring at my computer. I push away from my desk, desperate for a break, and my stomach growls. The clock on my computer reads four forty-nine pm. I worked through the day without lunch. I've barely eaten since Channing left. The grief has made my stomach a ball of nerves.

Since Channing's been gone, I've been going through the motions. Keeping my head down, working hard. Trying to forget how nice it felt to have him in the house.

In my bed.

In my heart.

How amazing it was to feel cared for. Loved. Protected.

But I sent him away, didn't I? The pleasure of having him didn't outweigh my fear of losing him.

I'm not sure that makes sense on a logical level, but it made sense in my heart at the time.

Now, I'm not so sure. Fear got the best of me. Not the best place to choose from.

I run down to the kitchen and grab a stalk of wilting celery. I chomp on that while I look through the fridge for what to make for dinner. I forgot to get groceries, so frozen pizza it is. Geo will be happy.

He hasn't been in a good mood for days. He won't admit it, but I know he's missing his uncle. My excuse that Channing's on a mission is wearing thin. At some point, I'll have to sit him down and explain that Channing is gone—this time for good.

I've avoided the conversation because a part of me doesn't want it to be true.

On the way back to my office, I pass by Geo's bedroom door, and it creaks open. Odd. It's late. He should be home by now, holed up in his room, doing homework.

Did he arrange to hang out with Justin and not tell me? I call Geo, but the call goes straight to voicemail.

I dial up Justin's mom.

Ten minutes later, I'm in a panic. Geo isn't at Justin's house. Nor is he at the school. In fact, Justin remembers Geo getting on the bus. I called the school, too, but the bus wasn't delayed.

I've called Geo several times and texted up a storm. Nothing.

I go into the app I have on his phone, the one I used to track him, but it circles around Flagstaff and doesn't pinpoint any location, like it's having trouble finding a signal. It might be a glitch, but I have a bad feeling about this.

Geo isn't home, and as far as I know he isn't with his friends. His phone is off, and the tracker isn't working. He could've come home and gone for a run or something without letting me know.

Would he do that?

I head out back and holler his name, until my voice echoes off the hill.

"Julia?" Buddy steps out front behind a pine tree. I can't see his whole body–it's obscured by a bush–but I can tell he's shirtless. Was he in animal form?

If he finds it awkward to converse with me while he's naked, he doesn't show it. I certainly don't care.

"Have you seen Geo?"

He shakes his head. In the past few days, he's grown a beard, and it's black with a white stripe down the center, like his hair. It reminds me of an animal pelt, but I can't place which one.

"What about his...scent?" I ask. "Can you tell if it's fresh? Did he get off the bus and come straight back here to run?"

"No," Buddy says. "He hasn't been here since this morning."

I nod, my insides deflating. Logically I knew there'd be evidence Geo stopped by the house before stripping to shift into wolf form. He'd leave his backpack and clothes, and there's no sign of them.

Did he sneak off to hunt for his Uncle Channing?

No, a small voice tells me. *He wouldn't do that without telling you.*

Which means something is wrong.

"He's missing," I tell Buddy. "I'm going to call Channing."

Buddy shuffles, but doesn't come out from behind the bush. "Do you want me to call?"

"No. Can you keep an eye out, in case Geo shows up?"

"Of course."

"Thanks." I head back into the house, hitting Channing's number before I'm inside. As soon as I do, relief hits me. I pushed Channing away because of the danger he brought, but suddenly it's so clear—in a crisis, he's the one I run to. The one I trust.

* * *

Channing

My phone buzzes, and I come awake, snapping upright. I ran in the Grand Canyon last night until my paws bled. I didn't make it back until mid-day when I stretched out on a picnic table in human form and must have fallen asleep. Finally.

My wolf is frantic, and I know something's wrong before I see the name of the caller.

"Julia?"

"Geo's missing," she says. "Is he with you?"

"What? No." I surge to my feet. "What do you mean missing?"

"He never came home from school. I thought he might have run away from home, gone to try to find you."

"He wouldn't do that. He wouldn't worry you like that."

"I know," her voice cracks.

"Wait a minute," she sounds distracted. "Someone's pulled up to the front door."

"Julia–wait–"

She's gone before I can warn her to check the peephole before unlocking the deadbolt. She's not stupid.

Even so, I pull up the view from the security cameras on my phone. There's a nondescript black sedan in Julia's driveway. The driver is a beefy looking guy in sunglasses.

I switch the camera view to the one of her doorway and my insides turn to cement.

There, on Julia's front stoop, is Hannibal.

* * *

Julia

The man on my stoop looks professional enough. He's in a suit that must be custom to fit his massive frame. The car in my driveway looks like the one that took me to the airport, but I can't be sure.

"Who is it?" I hesitate, my hands on the lock.

"Mrs. Armstrong?" a deep voice rumbles through the door. "Mr. van den Berg requests your presence at his home."

Why did my boss send a car for me? Did I forget something? I open the front door. "Now's not a good time."

"I think it is, Ms. Sanchez. He wanted me to tell you, he has your son."

"Geo." I sag against the door frame. "Thank goodness." Wait–but why? My brain tries to make sense of it. My boss must have picked him up for an outing. Or did it have something to do with the new school? I'm totally confused, but at least I know he's safe. "One second. Let me grab my purse." I turn–I left my phone on the side table with my keys. Channing is still on the other line. I can hear him yelling something.

"Julia! Don't–"

"You won't be needing that." The big guy closes his hand over my arm, pulling me back. Before I can snap at him to let me go, he plucks my cell phone off the table and crushes it in his fist.

I gasp, and he propels me out the door. "This way. Better not keep Mr. van den Berg waiting."

* * *

Channing

I watch in helpless fury as Hannibal drags Julia out the door and hauls her into the backseat of the car. My shouted warnings didn't reach her in time. Even if they had, what could she do against Hannibal? The fucker could overpower her with a finger.

I knew Mr. van den Berg was a creep. He has Geo–I overheard that much.

The sedan rolls beyond the scope of the cameras, but not before I clock a welcome sight. A furry black and white shape flowing down the driveway.

Buddy. He came through. If he tagged the car, we have a chance.

I hit the emergency button on my phone, radioing for back up. "Flagstaff. Location TBD."

If Buddy does his job, I'll have a location soon.

I hop on my bike. A few minutes into my ride, my phone buzzes with Buddy's call.

"Tell me you got it," I say by way of greeting.

"Tagged it." He's out of breath from chasing after the car and stealing away unseen. "I'll send you the location."

"Send it to command central, too." Buddy has a line to our pack headquarters. He'll communicate with them while I hunt Hannibal down.

"Done."

"I couldn't' stop them," he says, his voice soaked in regret. "I couldn't fight–"

"You did what you needed to do. We have a chance to save her and Geo because of you."

"Go get them," Buddy says.

"Ten four. Channing out."

I pull up the coordinates Buddy sent me. Hannibal's car is on the move, and I can guess where they're going.

Time to visit Julia's boss. I just need Geo and Julia to stay alive until I can pull off the rescue.

I rev my bike and zoom off at top speed.

Hang on, Julia. I'm coming.

* * *

Julia

The sun has sunk below the horizon by the time we pull into the long drive leading to Mr. van den Berg's mansion. I've been here before for a holiday party. The gothic architecture looked festive, strung with lights. Now the imported stone looks cold and forbidding as a stone fortress. A prison.

No one's explicitly said that I'm a prisoner, but what else would I be? A giant man forced me into the back of a car against my will. And he said they have my son.

I sit in silence, my posture stiff and upright. I'm in my work clothes–a V-necked sweater and yoga pants. No shoes, just my wooly house socks. No phone. No weapon.

I only have my wits and the knowledge that Channing will find me. If he didn't hear everything over the phone, Buddy will fill him in.

Channing will come for me. It seems his instincts about my boss were right. I should have listened. He'll move heaven and earth to rescue me and Geo. I need to sit tight, get to Geo and keep us alive until he comes.

I ask a few questions, keeping my voice calm. "What does Mr. van den Berg want with me? Why did he take Geo?"

The driver says nothing. Neither does the huge guy in the seat next to me, the one who forced me into the car. He catches me eyeing the door latch and lock.

"No," he rumbles. His voice is deep and wrong somehow. It makes me want to slam myself against the far door. "No funny business."

"I want to see my son," I tell him.

The car pulls up to the imposing front door–an arched monstrosity lined with statues–modeled after Notre Dame Cathedral. I wait for the big guy to exit and come around to open my door. He doesn't grab me this time. The bruises on my arm throb as I pass him and walk into the house.

My guide doesn't take me to one of the lovely sitting rooms or Mr. van den Berg's office off the massive library.

"This way." He herds me to a side door and opens it. Cold, stinking air hits my face. I shiver, staring down the stone staircase.

"I want to see my son," I say in a calm voice. No use panicking, even if I could. I'm in a place beyond panic, beyond fear. Nothing matters but getting to Geo.

He nods to the shadowy stairs. "Down." He'll hurt me if I don't go. The ache in my arm attests to that.

Geo, please be okay.

I take a breath of fresh air and descend. Lights blink to life as I pass. The stench isn't mold or like an underground drain. It's thick and reeking of blood and offal, like a meat processing plant. I breathe through my mouth as I tread deeper, my guard dogging my heels.

At the bottom of the stone stairs, the chill in the air bites through my thin sweater. My guard reaches past me to press a code onto the hi-tech looking keypad beside the heavy stone door.

The hallway beyond is something out of a nightmare. My feet freeze on slick stone floor. On either side of me are thick doors with bars on top of them. Prison cells.

Goosebumps race across my already chilled skin. Why does my boss have a dungeon in his basement? What kind of sick, twisted... Panic surges, and I shove it back down again. I need to stay calm for Geo.

My guard throws open one of the doors and pushes me inside.

Twin lights blink on in thick shadows. In front of me—a pair of eyes.

"Mom?" Geo surges to his feet and hugs me.

"*Mijo.*" I clutch him to me. There's no overhead light in here, but he feels unharmed. Whole.

Behind us, the prison door slams shut. The guard peers through the bars.

"Mr. van den Berg will be with you soon."

"Wait," I shout, but he's gone. "What's happening?" I ask Geo, running a hand over his head to reassure me he's there.

"I don't know. Mr. van den Berg pulled up and told me you were at his house, and he was supposed to pick me up. My wolf knew something was wrong, but a big guy snuck up behind me and stabbed my neck with a needle. I woke up here. But I'm fine."

The betrayal burns like acid in my throat. Mr. van den Berg insinuated himself into our lives. But why?

Once we escape, I will wring my boss' neck.

"We're going to get out of here," I tell Geo confidently. I don't mention Channing because there are cameras here, and I don't want them to know he's coming. "Can you pull out the bars?"

"I tried. They burn me."

Silver.

Oh my God. Mr. van den Berg knows Geo's a shifter. Is van den Berg a shifter, too? What does he want with us?

A distant bang, and the air shifts. Measured footsteps echo down the hall.

Lights blink on, beaming through the bars. I wince, squinting at the bright square of the door until a shadow falls over it.

"Julia. I'm so glad you're here." Mr. van den Berg's voice

is smooth as scotch, like he's greeting me at an afternoon meeting instead of in a dungeon.

I push Geo behind me, placing myself in van den Berg's line of sight.. "Why are we here? Why are you doing this? What do you want?"

"I'm so glad you asked." He steps back, revealing the giant guard behind him. He's in lecture mode. All he's missing is his damn drink. "For generations my family has been able to afford any pleasure money can buy. My grandfather used to take me on long hunting trips. He told me of his great-grandfather, who hunted all sorts of game in these forests. The biggest stags, bears and mountain lions you'd ever seen. These days, humans have driven out or killed all the natural predators. Do you know that huge wolves once roamed these hills? Now there's less than one hundred in the state."

"What does that have to do with us?"

"There's only one species that is still a threat to humans. Worthy of the hunt. One of my peers discovered them and founded an order to study them. I have recently been initiated into the order's ranks. And what did I find? A shifter living in my backyard." He leers at Geo.

"You targeted us." It makes sense. The cushy job, the flexible hours, the remote work. His unusual level of interest in our personal lives.

"I've been watching you both for some time. To my dismay, I couldn't get eyes inside your house. There was another security system in place and disturbing it would call attention to us."

Channing's security system. I never thought I'd be so grateful for it.

"But that was all right. Evidence said it would take years for Geo to be large enough to hunt. For his animal to emerge. To "get his wolf" as they say."

"You're a monster."

"No, my dear. I am a connoisseur. And your son is an animal. One me and my fellow Venatores will love to hunt. He will provide us with much entertainment in the coming weeks."

"Venatores? Is that what you call yourselves?"

"Has a nice ring to it doesn't it? And I will be their Premier, their Lanista, because I have secured the perfect prey. But we're having trouble getting Junior here to cooperate. He needed the right incentive. Hannibal?"

Van den Berg turns sideways. The giant leans forward, opening the door. He greets me with a pistol pointed at my chest.

"Geoffrey," Mr. van den Berg says. "If you don't want your mother to die, you will do as I say and shift."

* * *

Channing

Julia's boss lives in a big creepy house like the super villain he is. This is the kind of money behind Hannibal.

I meet Buddy on the edge of the manicured grounds overlooking a small parking lot. Three familiar-looking armored cars are parked there. Van De Butt must order them in bulk.

Buddy's in animal form, his big fluffy tail twitching. There's a long white stripe down his back signaling danger to anyone who would get on his bad side.

He's not much bigger than an ordinary skunk. Not in stature. But his spray can reach fifty feet. If it doesn't kill you, you'll wish it had.

"We're going in now." My wolf tells me I can't wait for backup. At least we're under the cover of darkness. "I need you to cut the power. Take out the lights, the electricity. If you can find the security system controls, make it go highwire. Sprinklers, everything. Chaos. It'll be my cover."

Buddy the skunk squeaks.

I hold out a tiny com. "Here. You'll be able to hear everything I'm doing. I'll let you know if orders change." The skunk rises on hind legs, and I tuck the tracker into his ear. I'll have to thank Lance later. He's the one who designed and engineered the rodent-sized communication device.

"And this." I hand him a special car-jacking tool I picked up on a black op. He pops it into his mouth, where it bulges in his cheek. "Drop that under an SUV for me, 'kay?" The tool will allow us to hack one of the smart cars. "If your life is threatened, you get out. You save yourself, understand?"

Instead of squeaking, he raises his tail. A threat.

He's telling me no, he'd rather complete the mission than get out alive.

I hold out my fist, surprisingly choked up. "Thanks, man. When we get out of this, you get all the chocolate covered bugs you want. On me."

He pops my fist with his paw, completing the world's tiniest fistbump and hustles away. I watch the bright white stripe zoom over the grass and disappear under the car. He'll take a moment and use my invention to prep a getaway vehicle for us before finding a way into Count Von Asshole's knock off villian fortress. He'll do some redecorating for me, causing the chaos I requested. Once I give word, he'll spray some air freshener. There's got to be guards and security systems in the house, but Buddy will help level the playing field.

Hannibal's in that house. And Geo. And Julia.

I clip my com in my ear and strip. Underneath my jeans and leather jacket I'm wearing the boxer briefs the Army engineered for us.

I shift and sneak over the grass expanses, my wolf low to the ground. I crouch behind the SUVs, finding Buddy's subtle scent marks–nothing pungent, just enough to leave me a breadcrumb trail, skunk-style.

The seconds tick by. The moon is a sliver over my head.

Across the way, the hum of the outdoor generators ceases. A minute later, every lit window in the mansion goes dark.

I spring towards the house.

* * *

Julia

I stare down the barrel of the pistol, my world narrowed to the black hole, and Geo's fragile warmth behind me.

A whine escapes Geo's throat, but nothing happens.

"I'm not a patient man," van den Berg growls. The weapon in my face wavers not a millimeter.

The light's flicker once, twice and wink out, plunging us into darkness.

The door in front of me swings shut.

"What is this? What's going on?" van den Berg whines like a child.

"Sir," says the big guy, Hannibal. "We need to get you out of here."

"No. Go, deal with it."

Hannibal stomps away.

I huddle with Geo at the far end of the cell. "*Mijo*, on my signal, I need you to shift."

"Mom, I can't. I've been trying."

"You can. You absolutely can. You're my son. Your father would be proud of you."

Geo lets out another whine, and I grip him harder. "I am proud of you. And so is Channing. He's here now, and he needs your help." Geo buries his face in my neck, his whole body trembling. I sense him going deep inside himself, communing with his wolf. For too long, he's been afraid of his animal. Ashamed that he was so different from his human friends. I might have contributed to that shame with my human fear. But I release it now.

Channing showed him the joy of what he is. With Channing, he exalted in his wolf nature. He found a whole new world. And then I shut it all down. But I was wrong. My son is a wolf. He needs to be with other wolves. And I need Channing.

There. I admitted it. I've been denying myself the one person who could change my entire world. Fill the cavernous void left by Geoffrey. Make things light and fun. Give me pleasure and companionship. Love.

All for what? Safety?

Look where that got me. We've never been less safe, and it's because Channing wasn't with us.

"I know you're in there," I whisper to the wolf. "You're a part of our family, and we need you right now." Geo will accept the beautiful monster inside him, and so will I.

Van den Berg raps the bars with his gun. "What are you saying over there? Stop it." He aims the gun at me. "You. Julia. Get up. I need a hostage."

I rise to my feet, murmuring, "Get ready, *mijo*."

The door swings open.

"Come," van den Berg waves me forward. I step into the hall, and dive to the right. A bullet whines past me and buries itself into the wall.

A growl echoes in the cell, and a ghostly shadow blasts through the open door. van den Berg screams. His weapon clatters on the floor. I grab it and rise.

A giant wolf stands over the still form of van den Berg, its jaws next to his face.

"Good work." I aim the gun, covering Geo as he steps over to me. van den Berg might be playing dead. "Let's go."

We make it back up the staircase unhindered. I close the doors behind us, hoping they will lock.

Geo's wolf lopes beside me. I keep a hand on his back, gripping the thick fur. The beast is strong and sturdy, something I can rely on.

A howl goes up in the distance. *Channing*. Geo's wolf

speeds forward, pulling me with him. I keep the gun up, alert, and trust my son to nose his way down the hall.

A second later he sneezes. I smell it, too. An eye watering stench, like someone let one hundred skunks in here.

Another howl, this one sounding closer. Channing's somewhere inside the house. We have to get to him. I can't go straight to the exit–it'll be guarded. We need to sneak out.

I lead us in the direction of the howl, until we come to a statue I recognize from the holiday house tour.

"This way." I nudge Geo to the right, through a library that smells of leather and ancient books. The side door leads to van den Berg's study. Ahead are the huge windows. I run to one and look down. We can pry it open and jump out that way. It's on the second floor, but there are some bushes below that can break our fall.

Voices sound in the hallway, and I drop behind the desk. Geo pushes next to me, panting.

"This way." van den Berg sounds peeved. Heavy boots tromp along with him. "Don't disturb the furniture," he snaps. "I'll be in my study. Find them and bring them to me."

The door to the study swings open. "I need a drink." My ex-boss marches to his minibar. I hold my breath.

Gunshots crack in a far part of the house. Boots rush in that direction. More gun fire.

Then, a low growl. Channing is getting closer.

Van den Berg curses. Ice clinks as he picks up a phone. "Yes, you fool, he's here." Van den Berg snaps to someone on the other line. "I can hear him killing your men."

"Must I do everything myself?" He slams down the

phone and heads to a case next to the fireplace. "I was going to hunt your nephew, but you are much more impressive."

More shouts. Bullets thud the walls. A roar shakes the room, followed by a piercing scream and a horrible squelch. A growl rumbles through the door.

Channing's outside.

van den Berg removes a shotgun from his private case and raises it, aiming at the door.

I rise up, and take a shooting stance. "Hey, asshole."

Van den Berg's head whips around.

"I quit." And I blow him away.

* * *

Channing

I hear a shot and burst through the door. A dead man lies prone on the carpet, holding a shotgun. Julia stands with both hands steady on a pistol, breathing hard.

Geo surges from behind the desk.

I shift back and go to them. "You okay? You hurt?"

"We're okay." Julia's eyes are wide. She's trembling and pale.

I crouch to check van den Berg. He's dead. I take his shotgun.

"I had to." Julia's voice quavers. "He was going to shoot you."

"I know. You did good. C'mere." I pull her into a hug. "You both did."

"There are more of them," her voice is barely a whisper.

Alpha's Command

"I know. I took out as many as I could. Buddy will take care of the rest."

"Buddy?" She wrinkles her nose.

"He's here. He'll cover our exit. We're getting out of here." I motion to the window.

Voices sound in the hallway. Geo's wolf charges to the window and leaps through while I shield Julia from the spray of glass. I scoop her up and jump down to the lawn. Geo and I streak towards the forest.

"All right, Buddy. Stink em up," I order into my comm.

We're almost to the parking lot when a roar blasts out backs. Hannibal stands in the ruined office window, framed in broken glass.

He's coming for us. With my shifter speed, I might be able to outrun him while carrying Julia, but I don't want to risk it. Hannibal could take out Geo and then focus on us.

I need to stand and face him.

"Change of plans," I bark to Geo. "Head to the SUV. Buddy, get out of there."

I put Julia down and reach a hand under the SUV, where Buddy left the carjacking tool. With it, I easily open the door and set it on the driver seat.

"Geo, shift back. You're driving."

"What?" Julia gapes. "Why wouldn't I drive?"

"Because," I guide her to the passenger seat and hand her the weapon I took off Van den Butt. "The shotgun rides shotgun."

"What about you?"

"I'm going to protect my family." I allow myself a moment to touch her cheek, then get out of Geo's way. "Keep your mom safe," I order him as he scrambles into the driver's seat. "I'm counting on you."

I turn and face the monster stalking towards us, horns growing out of his head.

* * *

Julia

Channing strides across the lawn, towards the mansion.

His gait is fluid and smooth as a wolf's while still being cocky as hell.

The huge guard, Hannibal, charges from the shadows. Huge horns top his head. His suit is fraying at the seams, ripping to shreds as monster bursts out of him. He looks like a demon, and he's running towards us.

Channing stands his ground. "Rematch!" he shouts. He gets a running start and his wolf explodes out of him, racing towards Hannibal. The two collide, and the earth shakes.

I grip the *oh shit* handle in the SUV, hanging onto the shotgun with the other. Channing and Hannibal are a blur of fur and horns.

"Got it," Geo mutters, fiddling with the device Channing used to unlock the car. The engine roars to life. He doesn't wait, just hits the gas. The SUV lurches for the forest. Since when does Geo know how to drive? Did Channing teach him? I'll ask later.

"Swing around," I order, gaining my balance and gripping the shotgun with both hands. It's loaded. "I want a clear shot."

"No." Geo's voice has dropped an octave since we spoke in the cell. "I have my orders. I'm getting you safe."

I crane my neck as we roll away. In front of the mansion, the horned beast thumps its fists down. He misses Channing and hits the ground. The earth craters and shockwaves surge under the car.

The next time, his fists find Channing. The white and brown wolf lunges away, its hind legs not working too well.

Hannibal stomps after the limping wolf.

A tiny furry body races out of the door and leaps, latching onto Hannibal's leg. The monster bellows and kicks. The little body goes flying.

"Buddy," I cry. The little body lies still fifty yards away from us. "We have to help him!"

"We have to go." Geo's voice cracks. "This is what he would want."

The wolf has recovered. It leaps again, snarling, engaging the horned monster in a deadly dance. But his teeth and claws do nothing to the monster. The only weapon Channing has against Hannibal is his speed.

I have to help him.

"*Mijo,*" I whisper. "Please. He's my mate."

Geo shakes his head, but he touches the brakes. The SUV slows.

I cup his cheek. "If anything happens to me, you run far and fast as you can. Shifter speed, okay? You can outrun anything."

Sobs shake Geo's shoulders as he nods.

"I love you," I tell him and slip out the SUV door.

***

Channing

I face Hannibal, my forepaws dragging myself upright. His foot caught me a minute ago and broke my back. My spine tingles with regenerative healing.

The odds aren't on my side for this fight. This fucker isn't a normal shifter. He's modified in some way. I've never met a shifter like him. Who can bounce a rocket off his chest and survive?

He's slower than I am, but I'm tiring. My teeth and claws can't penetrate his armor-like skin. I need a way to beat him.

The SUV rolls up, honking like it's stuck in NYC traffic. It screeches to a halt between Hannibal and Buddy.

What the hell?

"Hannibal," Julia shouts. She's standing on the lawn, frail and unprotected.

She racks the shotgun and aims. *Boom!*

Hannibal bellows. He took a direct shot, right to his chest.

Julia chambers another round and takes aim again. *Boom!* Another hit, and Julia's still upright. She took the recoil into her shoulder.

My brother would be proud.

Hannibal sways on his feet, shuddering. But he's still upright. How many rounds does that hunting shotgun have? Three? Five? I get the feeling Van De Butt would wait until his prey was wounded by his men before stepping in to deliver the final, killing shot.

Julia will be defenseless.

Alpha's Command

I roar and race towards Hannibal, but he's already headed for Julia. She stares him down, bracing the shotgun for what might be the final shot.

Boom! Hannibal staggers. She got him in the chest with what might be silver shot. Will that be enough to stop him?

I speed towards them. The world slows, blurring. Julia steadies the shotgun and aims for Hannibal's head. The gun recoils with the blast, but the bullet whines past Hannibal's horns. Missed.

Hannibal bellows and rushes Julia like an enraged bull. Her gun blasts off again. Hannibal's head twitches like he's been bit by a bug, but the bullet only grazed him. He keeps coming.

And she's out of shot. She's frozen, holding the gun like a club.

Beep beep! The SUV flies up out of nowhere and smashes into Hannibal. The front of it crumples, but Hannibal falls and stays down long enough for the SUV to reverse and head to pick up Julia. She jumps in the passenger seat.

I knew those secret evasive driving lessons I gave Geo would come in handy. I'll ask forgiveness later.

If I survive this fight.

Hannibal jerks upwards and lopes after the SUV.

I'm about to give chase, dog his heels, see if i can stop him, when the back of the SUV flies open. Buddy the skunk sticks his butt out of the trunk and raises his tail.

My wolf rolls and sticks its nose in the earth just in time. The stench blasts over the lawn.

Hannibal goes down, bellowing. His horns rake the earth as he buries his head to escape the smell.

The SUV rolls towards the forest. Buddy bought them some time, but Hannibal isn't down yet. As soon as he can, he'll be after them.

It's up to me to stop him.

I heave myself towards him, snorting and gagging on the reeking air. The wind picks up, and I lean into it, flying to Hannibal and knocking him to the ground. I pivot and race back, tearing at his arms, tiring him out. He's so much bigger, but I'm a wolf. And this is my family. No one touches them and lives.

I dart in, worrying him again and again. His fists find my still-healing back, but I roll away, escaping the force of the blow. I come round again, and he lowers his horns, goring me. I dance back, bleeding from gouges in my sides.

Hannibal surges to his feet, and I see an opportunity. The silver bullets did their damage. Black rot spreads across his chest, radiating from the pits of the gunshot wounds. If I'm lucky, the ruined skin will be enough to give my teeth purchase.

It's now or never. I run towards him, leaping at the last minute. My canines find the wasted skin, and I clamp my jaw down. The silver burns my gums and tongue and still I bite, driving my teeth deep.

Hannibal rains his fists onto my back. My spine snaps under the force. Pain blasts through me.

And still I hold on.

He smashes my shoulders and drags me back. I push but my back legs don't work. I grip my jaw tighter. Flesh tears from Hannibal's chest. I toss my head, spitting it, and clamp down again.

I have to protect my family.

Hannibal wrenches away, and I fall spent. But my bite did its work. His guts spill out, and he bows forward, holding them in. With a final roar, he rushes away.

I try to lift my head, but it barely moves. My whole body is a mass of fire. Blood soaks the ground around me.

"Channing." Lilac and lavender embrace me. Am I dreaming?

No. Julia's here, dropping to her knees beside me. "Ay, *Dios*."

Darkness rises, claiming me. But I wrench my head around, so she's the last thing I see.

Chapter Thirteen

Julia

I kneel on the grass beside Channing, hovering my hands over the bloodstained fur. I don't know where to touch him. Hannibal scored wounds up and down his sides. And broke as many bones as he could before he ran off.

The ground under my knees is wet and black.

"You can't die," I snarl, holding back a sob. "You just came back."

"Mom," Geo cries. He's trying to pilot the smashed SUV towards us, but it's too late. The mansion doors bang open and a stream of security guards come rushing out. I can only watch as they round the SUVs and head for us, guns out.

A brutal wind blows. A helicopter descends and hovers over us, its clacking blades loud enough to deafen. If it belongs to van den Berg, this is the end.

I bow over Channings' body. "I love you," I whisper over the rising winds.

A *rat tat tat* rips the air overhead. A figure in Army fatigues stands in the open side of the helicopter, manning a gun.

The bullets spray the oncoming forces, mowing them down. The gun does four passes, back and forth.

Once the helicopter is low enough to the ground, two figures leap out of the side and stride towards us. They're carrying machine guns and race across the ground until they're standing over us, giving us cover.

"Clear," one barks.

The helicopter sets down nearby, and the rushing wind dies.

"Ms. Sanchez?" The closest soldier offers me a hand. "I'm Rafe Lightfoot." I recognize the name. This is Channing's alpha.

"Nice to meet you," I say but don't take Rafe's hand. I don't dare to move, in case Channing is dying. There's a little rise and fall of his furry chest.

A blond guy winks at me. "I'm Lance Lightfoot. That's Deke." He nods towards his third packmate, a huge guy clad all in black, who's still pointing the gun. "And Teddy flew us in. Channing, you did good!"

"He's hurt," I choke out.

"Cover us," Rafe orders his brother, who snaps into a serious shooting stance. Rafe leans down, studying Channing for a moment.

"No silver bullets. No crushed skull. He's fine. He'll heal soon." He shakes his head. "Channing, quit freaking out your lady."

Alpha's Command

I turn and get a face full of wolf tongue. "Ah!" I cry as he licks my face.

I'm laughing as Channing shifts back. His left arm hangs a little funny, but he pulls me to him with his right one until I'm on his lap.

"You're hurt." I squirm, not wanting to lean my weight on him.

"I'm fine." He slants his head, pulling me in for a hard kiss. Under my butt, his cock stirs. He just took a beating, and he's still down to bone.

Unbelievable.

"That's what I'm talking about," Lance whoops. "Yeah boy!"

Channing breaks the kiss, and I lean against him, too spent to care.

"Hannibal," Channing says, turning his head slowly, like it's stiff. "Did I get him?"

"He ran away," I say.

Channing curses.

"It's okay," I cup his cheek. "You beat him."

"He's not dead. Fucker's hard to kill."

"Everything can die. It's just a matter of finding his weak spot." Rafe sounds like he's personally going to find Hannibal's Achilles' heel and hunt him down. "We'll deal with that another day."

"You want me to clear the mansion?" Lance asks. "Deke and I can go."

"Uhhhh..." Channing says.

"Fuck," mutters Deke, joining us. "What's that stench?"

"That's Buddy." Channing must be feeling better

because he nods easily towards Geo and the SUV. "He was my backup."

"Buddy?" demands Lance. "Surveillance guy buddy? Doesn't like to fight, pacifist Buddy?"

Channing shrugs. "He drinks, and he stinks. That Buddy."

"Consider the mansion clear," Rafe says. "I've called in more air support. I'm thinking a house fire got out of control, destroyed the place. A gas line blew, and it burned so hot, no bodies were found."

"Tragic." Channing grins, flashing those dimples I love so much.

"Wait," I say. "Van den Berg said something about an order. There are more of them. They called themselves Venatores."

"Venatores?" Rafe strokes his chin.

"We need to get the records. There might be information on the computers or down in the dungeon."

"Dungeon?" Lance repeats.

"Later," Channing says. "I want to get my family," he gives me a heated look, "home safe."

"Do it," Rafe says. "We'll debrief later."

Channing rises and pulls me to my feet while I fuss over him.

"Careful," I say, but he dips and tosses me over his shoulder.

I squawk and pound his taut butt until he sets me down. Geo crashes into his uncle, and Channing pulls us into a group hug.

Buddy waves at us from the back seat of the SUV.

"That was epic," Geo shouts. "You were like *rrrrr*, and he was like *roar!* And then I smashed into him—"

"Great work, kid." Channing thumps Geo's back. "You did great. Let's get you a change of clothes."

Geo pops his head up. "Hey, Mom, can I drive home?"

"No!" I look at Channing, shaking my head.

"I have an idea." Channing's dimples reappear. "Have you ever ridden in a helicopter?"

"Please. Can we just Uber?" I laugh.

* * *

Channing

In the end, I borrow an armored SUV and drive Julia and Geo back home, after Teddy pulled a bag from the helicopter and gave Geo and me some clothes. Buddy declined a ride, saying he wanted to help sack the mansion.

On the drive home, I get a call from Rafe on a burner phone he handed me. Kylie's already called dibs on Van De Butt's computer systems. From what they've found in the house, it looks like there's evidence of a widespread network of Venatores, but we need to know more.

"That's a fight for another day," Rafe says. "You did good, soldier. Hold the fort at home. Be with your family. That's an order."

"Yes, sir."

I see Geo listening intently, his back straightening a little at the *sir*, and I realize perhaps I do have something to offer as a father figure. Something Geoffrey would have given him.

"I joined the military because of your dad." I glance in

the rearview mirror to catch his eyes. "Because I wanted to be the kind of male he was. Someone with honor and courage."

"You are that man–male," Julia says. She reaches over and squeezes my hand. I lift her fingers to my lips and kiss them. "I'm sorry I drove you away," she murmurs, apparently not minding that Geo can hear. "I am still terrified for your safety and Geo's, but you being gone was no solution. I was trying to protect my heart, but it was no less painful than if something had happened to you."

I pull up in front of her house, and Geo tumbles out and bolts for the door, probably to give us some privacy.

"Julia." I turn off the vehicle and twist in my seat to face her. "I know I can't take Geoffrey's place."

"I don't want Geoffrey," she blurts, and my brows fly to my hairline. "I mean Geoffrey's dead. I want you, Channing. Reckless, loveable you. I don't need you to be like Geoffrey or anyone else."

I try and fail to swallow around the constriction in my throat. "Yeah?" I rasp.

"Definitely. I want you." She holds my gaze, and my stomach flops then begins to warm, sending a heat through my entire trunk.

I don't know why I still can't believe it. "You want me?" I point at my chest.

Julia blinks back moisture in her eyes. "Will you stay, Channing? Please?"

I throw open the door and tear around the SUV, not even bothering to close my door. I practically rip her door from the hinges in my haste to get it open.

"Come here." I scoop her out of the SUV, and she wraps her legs around my waist, dropping kisses along my forehead as I carry her inside.

I hear Geo in the shower upstairs, so I carry her to the downstairs bathroom where I set her down only long enough to strip her of her clothes.

"You haven't answered me yet," she says as I shuck my shifter briefs and turn on the water in the shower.

I laugh. "Are you really not sure? You think there's anything in this world I wouldn't do for you?"

She doesn't smile back. Her gaze travels over my healing wounds. The dried blood that stains my skin. Her brown eyes are filled with warmth.

I open the shower door and tip my head toward it, but she doesn't move.

"Mark me."

I go still, my dick punching out like a rod. For a moment, I can't speak. They are two words I never thought I'd hear her say. Never even allowed myself to hope for. Never thought I'd be worthy of.

"Are you sure?" I barely get the words out. My voice wobbles like a fucking pansy's.

"I'm sure. I want to be yours, Channing. Claimed by you. Marked. Married. I want you to stay. Or...seeing as how I'm out of a job—we could go somewhere else. Maybe to Taos? So Geo could join a shifter community?"

Fates help me, I want to fall to my knees and weep like a baby. Instead I walk over and pick up my woman, carry her into the shower where I pin her against the wall and deliver a searing kiss.

"I want you, Channing," she whispers when I break the kiss.

"Fuck." Not my most eloquent moment, but I'm beyond speech. Beyond belief. I kiss down her neck. Flick my tongue over her breasts. I crouch down to lift one of her knees and taste her.

Holding her pelvis pinned against the tile, I abuse her with my tongue, penetrate her, lap and lave her.

She grips my head, moans. Cries out. Pulls my mouth closer. I work her clit with the tip of my tongue, manage to get it between my lips to suck. She bucks. I screw two fingers inside her to stroke her inner wall as I suck and she comes, her juices flowing onto my tongue.

"Mark me."

Fuck.

I stand and turn, quickly soaping under the spray of water, wanting to be sure I'm clean for her. Worthy of my beautiful mate.

I have grand plans to turn off the shower and carry her to the bed, but she reaches for my cock, and I forget my own name.

I crowd against her, lift one of her knees to my waist and press in. I'm instantly lost.

Instantly found.

Instantly hers.

The entirety of my life spins and collapses to become nothing more than this moment. This pinnacle. This ecstatic opening.

I'm not sure what happens next. Me plowing into her. The two of us moving together. Crying out together. She's saying something, but I can't catch the words. She's chanting something.

Oh. Oh, Fates.

"IneedyouIneedyouIneedyouIneedyou."

My favorite words.

"You have me," I croak.

And then it all happens at once. My climax. Hers. My teeth snapping down and scoring the place where shoulder meets neck. She screams. We keep moving. Keep dancing. I keep thrusting until it's over. Until we both finish coming. Until I've licked her wounds closed and kissed all the flesh around it.

"I'm sorry," I croon. "I'm so sorry. I know it hurts."

"It's okay," she whispers. "I'm okay. It feels good. I mean, right." She nods, her head wobbly. "It feels right."

* * *

Julia

Channing stands out on my deck grilling hamburgers. Shirtless, as usual. We invited over his pack members, so Buddy, Rafe, Lance, Deke, and Teddy are gathered outside, too, talking in loud, friendly voices. Giving each other shit. Laughing.

I'm in the kitchen putting together a salad when Geo comes in from outside. "Need any help, Mom?"

I overheard Channing prompt him to come in and ask me, but even so, my heart melts. Because Geo is so transformed. That awkward, defensive middle school persona has dropped away.

He seems more comfortable in his skin.

Or maybe it's the fur.

I strongly suspect Geo's comfort is about finding his wolf and feeling part of a pack. Despite the terror of last night, I've never seen Geo so bright. He loved the dramatic action. Thrived on it, really.

"Can you get some napkins and paper plates out? And stay here, I wanted to talk to you for a minute." I look over my shoulder, so I can make eye contact. "Channing and I..."

"I know," he cuts in. "He claimed you."

I nod. "You can tell?"

"Yeah."

"Mom, I'm okay with it."

"With what?"

"You and Uncle Channing. I think it's good. He's great."

My legs give out under me with relief. "Sweetheart, no one will replace your dad, but—"

"It's okay. I like you two together."

"Thanks, *mijo*." I set a red onion on the cutting board and start slicing it for the burgers. "So that brings me to the next topic."

Geo comes over and leans against the counter. "What, Mom?"

"It's not something we have to decide right this second. It's just something I'd like you to think about. Do you want to stay here in Flagstaff, or should we move to Taos to be with Channing's pack?"

I expected Geo to balk at leaving his friends. Getting him to agree to change schools had been a major endeavor. But it seems Geo knows his own mind. "Taos. Definitely."

I suck in a surprised breath. There's a buoyancy in my chest. Around Geo.

"Yeah?" I set down my knife and wrap Geo in a tight hug.

Instead of pushing me away the way he's been doing over the last year or two, he chuckles and pats me awkwardly on the back. "Is that what you want, too?"

"Well, I think a change might be good for us. A fresh start after everything we've been through." I mean more than what happened with van den Berg. I mean losing Geoffrey. The loneliness and isolation I experienced, in addition to the love.

I release Geo as Channing comes in with a platter piled high with burgers and the five men follow behind, making the house feel absolutely tiny.

I wave them toward the plates, buns, and hamburger fixings on the center island. "Geo and I talked, and we'd like to move to Taos with you," I blurt.

"Yeah?" Channing's face breaks into a broad grin.

"That's great," Rafe says. "We were hoping you would say that. Not that I planned on letting Channing off the team. But we'd miss the fuu-*dge* out of having him on base." Rafe corrects his language at the last second. His gaze sweeps over Geo. "It'd be good to have some young blood around, too."

"Absolutely not," I say immediately. "I mean, nothing dangerous. Not my kid." I set the salad on the center island with the rest of the fixings.

Rafe assembles three hamburgers. "Of course not. He's

under my watch. The pack will protect him—and you—with our lives."

I suck in a breath. I still hate the idea of the danger they take on. I can't even think about losing Channing like I lost Geoffrey. But after seeing how badly-injured Channing was and yet, how quickly he recovered, I do feel better.

And I can't deny him what he is—a thrill-seeking warrior who will probably always make me nervous. Still, I can live with that anxiety. It's far better than the alternative. I never want to relive those horrible hours after I told Channing to leave. When I made the biggest mistake of my life.

As if he guesses at my thoughts, he loops an arm around my waist and pulls me against his rock-hard abs. "Geo's far safer in a pack," Channing murmurs, and I nod.

My gut had already told me that.

"I'll watch this place for you if you decide to keep it," Buddy offers.

"We're keeping it," Channing says firmly, then looks at me with his brows lifted. "I mean, I think we should. These are good running grounds. And the house reminds me of Geoffrey."

My eyes mist. "Will we need the money to buy a house in—"

Channing shakes his head. "I have plenty of money."

"Okay. Great." That takes some of the urgency off me finding a new job. Maybe I can return to non-profit work now. I turn and look at Buddy. "Would you be willing to stay here? I would want someone living in it."

Buddy perks right up. "Hell, yeah! I mean, heck, yeah! I'd totally stay here."

"Beats sleeping in your burrow, right?" Channing grins.

I wrinkle my nose and frown, trying to understand if he means it literally or figuratively. "Wait...have you been sleeping on my property in your, um, animal form?"

"Only because Channing paid me to keep an eye on things over here." Buddy shrugs. "And it's cheaper than owning a house." He tilts his head to the side. "I live out of my car."

A multitude of questions surge to the surface, like where and how he showers, but I dismiss them for another time.

"Welcome to the pack," Lance says just before he takes a giant bite of hamburger. "Both of you."

Deke grunts his agreement with the sentiment.

Geo grins back, more comfortable with a room full of adults than I've ever seen him.

"Thank you. Thanks for coming to save my son," I say, suddenly teary.

Channing pulls me against his side and kisses the top of my head.

"Always," Rafe says. The rest of the group murmur their agreement between bites.

I'm not a shifter, but even I feel an ease with this group of near-strangers. Secure in the knowledge that without knowing me, without anything more than the fact that I'm Channing's mate, they would welcome me in, give me the shirts off their backs. Lay down their lives for me.

This is what it means to have family. What I've been so desperately missing. It's the reason I resented Channing's absence.

Now I have everything I could ever ask for: Channing.

My son's self-actualization. A new family. Hopefully a return to the kind of work I loved–non-profit law. A fresh start.

Channing hands me a plate of food he filled for me. Like always, he's paying attention. Taking care of me. This gorgeous, wild, and a little goofy man chose me to be his mate.

I've never felt so loved.

So lucky.

Epilogue

Julia

The wind ruffles my skirts as I hike up the trail. I'm huffing and puffing, grateful for my hiking boots.

"You didn't have to wear a dress." Channing holds my arm to steady me.

"I wanted to," I tell him. The flowy white fabric is perfect for the warm day. The hand-embroidered flowers and off-the-shoulder design make me feel pretty. "We didn't have to hold the ceremony on top of a mountain, either."

"It's only a big hill. You want me to carry you?"

"Don't you dare," I warn, but I'm laughing, and he takes it as encouragement.

He scoops me up, flowy dress and hiking boots, floral headdress and all, and powers up the hill. I arrive at my own wedding in the groom's arms.

Channing's whole pack is here with their mates. Lance holds his little girl. Sadie leans against her big mate, Deke, who's wrapped his long arms around her to cup her belly. I bet there'll be more babies in the pack by this time next year.

Geo comes to greet us, looking amazing in his tux.

"Nice penguin suit." Channing claps Geo on the back.

"Stop," I say. "*Mijo*, you look so grown up."

"You have the rings?" Channing asks.

Geo nods solemnly.

Tears prick my eyes. "I'm not going to cry," I tell Adele, who laughs softly. She's holding my bouquet. In the last couple of months, she and I have become fast friends. She's the one who helped me secure a legal position with the Taos Pueblo. I have no idea how she hiked up here in her gorgeous high heeled boots.

"Ready to start?" Rafe asks, taking charge. He nods to Buddy, who's gotten certified to act as our officiant. Buddy cleaned up well. The tux sets off his white and black hairstyle beautifully.

"Wait." I turn to Channing, whispering even though all the shifters can hear me anyway. "I want to see it."

So Channing leads me to the lone pine tree standing amid the boulders. "Here." He crouches and points to the old scratch marks on a bare patch in the bark. Beside it are fresh scratches. "Geo made those this morning," Channing says. "But the old ones are Geoffrey's."

I lean down and put my hand over the marks, old and new, and give a prayer of thanks. *Thank you, Geoffrey, for your love. We continue on the foundation you gave us, a family you would be proud of.*

The wind picks up and lifts my hair. I rise with a sense of peace and take Channing's hand.

"Is this why you wanted to get married up here?" I ask.

He shrugs. "I only found that this morning," he tells me. "I chose this place because of the view."

It's not until we're standing up with Buddy in front of our friends and family do I see this special view Channing is talking about. We've hiked high enough to see the mountains in the distance, but that's not what draws the eye. At the foot of the hill, nestled in the pine trees, is my house. The house Geoffrey bought. The house where we became a family– Geoffrey, Geo, Channing and I. Where I lived with and lost one mate and then found another. The place where I raised my son. It's been a place of love and laughter, peace and contentment.

We kept it because it was a link to Geoffrey. To the past. But we've moved on.

Channing is my future.

My new home.

My family.

NEW Series Werewolves of Wall Street!

Chapter 1

B<i>rick</i>
The view from the Moon Co.'s executive suite would make a lesser man, a human, dizzy. The building is so tall, it sways in the wind. But that's the price of tasting rare air, and having all of Lower Manhattan at your feet.

Up here, it's easy to forget you're mortal. Up here, it's easy to feel like a god.

A shadow falls across the glass as Billy, my second in command, comes to stand beside me.

"We're almost there," he says quietly. I know he's referring to the vow we made years ago, in our dorm at Yale, on the worst day of my life. The day my father was murdered and our enemies destroyed everything he'd built.

"Almost," I growl. We both stare at the building across from us. The building our enemies erected to taunt us.

"We're close." He claps his hand on my shoulder. "The Adalwulfs won't know what hit them."

I pivot and take a seat at the head of the conference room table. Billy heads to open the door, to signal that the meeting is about to start. The rest of the executive team starts to file in.

That's when it hits me. A sweet scent, both bright and citrus-y but complex like nutmeg. Mouthwatering.

It's on the tip of my tongue to cuss and ream someone out. Perfumes and colognes of any type are banned from the premises. It's stated clearly in the employee handbook, practically on the first page. Billy takes great joy in firing the new hires that forget.

But it's not perfume. It's someone's natural scent. But whose?

There, by the elevator.

New Girl.

I fired my assistant Friday, which means her assistant, Indira, moved up the ladder, and there's a new starry-eyed college grad in Indira's place.

Alpha's Command

A young woman coolly surveys the top floor. She's no different than any other administrative assistant. Young, professional. She has a short dark brown bob and bold red lipstick.

But her scent.... I pull it through my nostrils, savoring the flavor.

Nutmeg and oranges. Maybe a hint of something exotic, like Frankincense.

"Who's that?" Billy flops down in his chair and leans back, making it balance on the last two legs, a display of strength no human could pull off. At my glare, he lets the chair fall to all four legs with a thump. "Your new secretary's secretary?"

He was there when I fired my former assistant Friday. I go through assistants like Billy goes through hookups.

"Must be."

"You want me to call her in?" he asks.

"Yes." Normally, I would say no. Normally, I wouldn't give her the time of day until I wanted something. But I need to examine that scent up close.

Billy looks at Indira and points at New Girl. He makes a beckoning motion, like he's irritated that Indira didn't already come in to introduce her. He's almost as skilled as I am at making employees jump and tremble with fear.

New Girl doesn't look afraid, though. I watch as she follows Indira in. As soon as I get a nose-full of her scent, I want to lick her from toe to clit.

Odd reaction to a human.

She's not even pleasing to the eye. I mean, she's pretty, but there's nothing soft and yielding about her. Something in the carriage of her neck, the lift of her chin, in the way she doesn't flinch when I glare in her direction, makes her look like she has a chip on her shoulder. With ten years added to her, she'd look like one of those power executive types. A female powerhouse, born to dominate every office. I employ a handful of women like her. You have to be strong to make it around here.

She assesses me right back, somehow managing to appear respectful and receptive, yet completely unafraid, even though it's her first day here.

Part of me wants to rip her a new one right from the start. Especially because I heard her murmur to Indira, "So that's the Big Bad Boss" before they walked in. Of course, she couldn't know that there's no conversation out of my hearing range on this floor.

The closer she gets, the more her scent infiltrates my senses. It's too pleasing to make me want to attack. Fates, is my dick getting hard?

I stand. "You are?"

"Mr. Blackthroat, this is–" Indira begins.

"Madison Evans." New Girl sticks her hand out for me to shake, saying her name at the same time as Indira. She meets my gaze steadily. There's no challenge to it, just attentiveness. She's reading me. I want to find something to criticize, but I can't. She's the right mixture of confidence and humility. Not overly bold, not cowering. There's something annoyingly appealing about her manner.

I already hate her. I accept her handshake. Her skin is soft. For some reason, my thoughts flick to the fact that her scent will now be on my palm. Not that I'm going to review it later.

"I go by Madi."

"I will call you Madison, *if* I remember your name. I'll expect you to answer to Assistant, Secretary, New Girl or whatever else I hurl at you at the moment." I release her hand.

Far from being taken aback, I see a trace of amusement in her expression. "I will answer to all of those," she assures me with a bow of her head.

"Good. Now take our coffee orders." I flick a brow like she should have already known to do this even though it's her first day. To Indira, I say, "Where are the financial reports?"

* * *

Madi

Rule number one of dealing with a Wall Street alpha-hole: Don't show weakness.

Blackthroat is staring at me. He's more good-looking and intimidating than the rest of them put together. His sleek suit accentuates the width and breadth of his powerful shoulders and chest.

I raise my chin and meet his gaze square on. "What kind of coffee can I bring you, sir?"

His eyes are dark. He's got a close clipped beard, and the lines around his eyes make him look older than his thirty-some years.

The second stretches to infinity. Mr. Blackthroat's glare

intensifies. For a moment, a bright sheen flares around his pupils. Must be a trick of the light.

"Triple Espresso." The deep growl of his voice wraps around my body and squeezes me.

I nod.

I'm still reeling from the fact that I am working for *the* Brick Blackthroat. Or, rather, Blackthroat's assistant, Indira.

My boss is the same age I am—just out of undergrad. She told me *her* boss got fired Friday, and she was bumped up the line. She's only been here three weeks total, herself.

At the moment, she is hurrying around her desk area, picking up and searching through folders. I suspect she doesn't even know what reports he's talking about.

It's probably some kind of test.

Well, I'll make sure we pass it right after I handle their coffee orders.

I don't plan on either of us getting fired today.

Or tomorrow.

Good thing I know how to navigate the waters of the one percent of the one percent.

Rule number two: act as if you belong.

So I pretend I'm not unnerved by the six good-looking assholes in ten thousand dollar suits sitting around a giant table. I recognize them as members of the executive team. I memorized the employee roster, as well as the three hundred and fourteen page handbook on the way to work this morning.

Rule number three: Always be prepared.

"I'll have a large red-eye, extra cream, no sugar," an exec says in the Queen's English. He must be Nicholas

Cavendish, the seventh. "Nickel" transferred from Oxford to Yale, Blackthroat's alma mater.

Then there's Vance Blackthroat, CFO. A cousin to the king. He doesn't even look up from his laptop. "Flat white. Tall."

"You aren't going to write this down?" William "Billy" White wears a smirk, like he thinks I'm about to bomb this test. He sports dimples in his cheeks and chin and has *player* written all over him.

"No, I'll remember," I assure him brightly. I'm not using a pen and paper or entering it into a text on my phone as a matter of pride. I have an excellent memory and intend to keep it honed, even if all I'm doing with my Princeton degree is serving a bunch of entitled assholes their coffee. I use the memory device of picturing me setting each paper cup with the label printed with their exact drink in front of them.

"Okay," he says slowly. "I'll have a caramel ribbon crunch Frappuccino with whip."

"Got it." I look politely at the next guy, but Billy interrupts, changing his mind. "No, actually, make that a tall, decaf mocha with only two pumps of chocolate."

I take two more orders when he changes it again. "Wait, hold up. I'd like a large latte breve with an extra shot. Got it?" The cocky bastard has the nerve to wink.

"Got it." I turn politely to get the last of the orders and leave the conference room.

I find Indira frantically clicking the mouse at her computer. "I had to get IT to get my former boss' password. Hopefully I can find the reports he needs. Are you okay to get the coffees? Just hit the cafe outside the building."

"No problem. Good luck with the reports. I'll be right back."

Ten minutes later, I'm down the block waiting in line to place the order. I should have ordered ahead on the app. I try not to get fidgety about getting raked over the coals for taking so long. There's nothing I can do at this point except apologize if I'm called out.

When I finally make it back with the two loaded trays of drinks, I have to set one of the carriers on the floor to open the door to the conference room.

Indira's inside, handing out the reports.

I serve the coffees, and Billy says, "What is this? Where's my flat white?"

My mind spins as I try to figure out if he's screwing with me.

He's frowning like he's pissed, but I catch a lip-twitch from Vance.

He *is* screwing with me. He totally is.

I'm sure of it when he says, "You really should have written down the orders." He shoots a glance in the direction of Blackthroat, as if he's a hunting dog delivering a tasty morsel at his master's feet.

I'm the morsel in this scenario.

"No, I'm good. I've got them all up here." I tap my temple. "You ordered a caramel ribbon crunch Frappuccino with whip, then changed it to a tall, decaf mocha with only two pumps of chocolate and then a large latte breve with an extra shot." I wait a beat before I say, "But I'm happy to go back and get you something else." There may or may not be a tinge of snark in my tone. I lean my hip against the giant, thick slab of polished mahogany that makes up the table. "Or were you just trying to trip me up? It takes more than a coffee order to confuse me."

He doesn't smile, but I hear a snort from across the table and a light chuff of laughter from Vance.

I reach across the table to adjust Billy's coffee cup, so the label faces him. "Were you a bully in high school, too?"

The very serious, professional, haughty looking execs suddenly turn into frat boys in a lounge. Or maybe that's what they've always been, but the suits deceived me. "Ohhhhh, she's a mouthy one," one of them cackles. "Serves you right," Nickel says.

"Are you going to let her get away with that?" Billy turns to Mr. Blackthroat.

What the actual F? Compared to the corporate culture I've seen everywhere outside of the board room, the familiarity within this group shocks me. But then, Blackthroat formed the start-up with his cousins and friends from college, so I suppose it makes sense.

"Am I going to let my *secretary's secretary* hand you your ass when you try to slip her up?" Blackthroat folds his arms across his chest.

Dear Lord, they are very fine arms, thick and corded with muscle. "Yeah, I guess I am." He turns to me. "Sit in the corner with Indira, that memory could be useful."

I find Indira seated in the shadowed corner by the door and pull up a rolling office chair beside her. "At first I thought I was being sent to the corner as punishment," I murmur under my breath.

She rolls her lips inward to keep from smiling.

Mr. Blackthroat's gaze flicks to me for a moment, and my belly flips. I doubt he heard me. My flutters have nothing to do with fear over losing my job. It's more like... excitement over his attention.

Score one for the assistants.

Big Bad Boss: Midnight

RULE #1 OF WALL STREET: DON'T HUNT WHAT YOU CANNOT EAT.

I'm the king of the business world. The Alpha of my pack. No one dares challenge me.

Except my new assistant.

She questions me to my face and calls me Big Bad Boss behind my back. When I give her an order, she asks me why, with all my billions, I can't afford some manners.

Worse, the little human smells like temptation. She dresses to kill, and I want to sink my teeth into her.

One day my control's going to snap, and a wolf never stops hunting until he's claimed his prey.

Midnight is book one in the Big Bad Boss *trilogy. It features a billionaire boss-hole wolf shifter and his freakishly smart assistant set in the* Bad Boy Alpha *world created by Renee Rose and Lee Savino.*

Preorder Big Bad Boss: Midnight now!

Want FREE books?

Go to http://subscribepage.com/alphastemp to sign up for Renee Rose's newsletter and receive a free books. In addition to the free stories, you will also get special pricing, exclusive previews and news of new releases.

Download a free Lee Savino book from www.leesavino.com

Read all the Midnight Romance Books

Bad Boy Alphas Series
Alpha's Temptation
Alpha's Danger
Alpha's Prize
Alpha's Challenge
Alpha's Obsession
Alpha's Desire
Alpha's War
Alpha's Mission
Alpha's Bane
Alpha's Secret
Alpha's Prey
Alpha's Sun

Shifter Ops Series
Alpha's Moon
Alpha's Vow
Alpha's Revenge

Read all the Midnight Romance Books

Alpha's Fire
Alpha's Rescue
Alpha's Command

Midnight Doms Series
Alpha's Blood by Renee Rose & Lee Savino
Her Vampire Master by Maren Smith
Her Vampire Prince by Ines Johnson
Her Vampire Hero by Nicolina Martin
Her Vampire Bad Boy by Brenda Trim
Her Vampire Rebel by Zara Zenia
Her Vampire Obsession by Lesli Richardson
Her Vampire Temptation by Alexis Alvarez
Her Vampire Addiction by Tabitha Black
Her Vampire Lord by Ines Johnson
Her Vampire Suspect by Brenda Trim

His Captive Mortal by Renee Rose & Lee Savino

The Vampire's Captive by Kay Elle Parker
The Vampire's Prey by Vivian Murdoch
Her Vampire Assassin by Erin St. Charles
Her Vampire Knight by Ines Johnson
All Souls Night - a Halloween anthology

Other Titles by Renee Rose

Made Men Series

Don't Tease Me

Don't Tempt Me

Don't Make Me

Chicago Bratva

"Prelude" in Black Light: Roulette War

The Director

The Fixer

"Owned" in Black Light: Roulette Rematch

The Enforcer

The Soldier

The Hacker

The Bookie

The Cleaner

The Player

The Gatekeeper

Alpha Mountain

Hero

Rebel

Warrior

Vegas Underground Mafia Romance

King of Diamonds

Mafia Daddy

Jack of Spades

Ace of Hearts

Joker's Wild

His Queen of Clubs

Dead Man's Hand

Wild Card

Contemporary
Daddy Rules Series

Fire Daddy

Hollywood Daddy

Stepbrother Daddy

Master Me Series

Her Royal Master

Her Russian Master

Her Marine Master

Yes, Doctor

Double Doms Series

Theirs to Punish

Theirs to Protect

Holiday Feel-Good

Scoring with Santa

Saved

Other Contemporary

Black Light: Valentine Roulette

Black Light: Roulette Redux

Black Light: Celebrity Roulette

Black Light: Roulette War

Black Light: Roulette Rematch

Punishing Portia (written as Darling Adams)

The Professor's Girl

Safe in his Arms

Paranormal

Two Marks Series

Untamed

Tempted

Desired

Enticed

Wolf Ranch Series

Rough

Wild

Feral

Savage

Fierce

Ruthless

Wolf Ridge High Series

Alpha Bully

Alpha Knight

Step Alpha

Bad Boy Alphas Series

Alpha's Temptation

Alpha's Danger

Alpha's Prize

Alpha's Challenge

Alpha's Obsession

Alpha's Desire

Alpha's War

Alpha's Mission

Alpha's Bane

Alpha's Secret

Alpha's Prey

Alpha's Sun

Shifter Ops

Alpha's Moon

Alpha's Vow

Alpha's Revenge

Alpha's Fire

Alpha's Rescue

Alpha's Command

Midnight Doms

Alpha's Blood

His Captive Mortal

All Souls Night

Alpha Doms Series

The Alpha's Hunger

The Alpha's Promise

The Alpha's Punishment

The Alpha's Protection (Dirty Daddies)

Other Paranormal

The Winter Storm: An Ever After Chronicle

Sci-Fi

Zandian Masters Series

His Human Slave

His Human Prisoner

Training His Human

His Human Rebel

His Human Vessel

His Mate and Master

Zandian Pet

Their Zandian Mate

His Human Possession

Zandian Brides
Night of the Zandians
Bought by the Zandians
Mastered by the Zandians
Zandian Lights
Kept by the Zandian
Claimed by the Zandian
Stolen by the Zandian
Rescued by the Zandian

Other Sci-Fi
The Hand of Vengeance
Her Alien Masters

Also by Lee Savino

Paranormal romance

The Berserker Saga and Berserker Brides (menage werewolves)

These fierce warriors will stop at nothing to claim their mates.

Draekons (Dragons in Exile) with Lili Zander (menage alien dragons)

Crashed spaceship. Prison planet. Two big, hulking, bronzed aliens who turn into dragons. The best part? The dragons insist I'm their mate.

Bad Boy Alphas with Renee Rose (bad boy werewolves)

Never ever date a werewolf.

Tsenturion Masters with Golden Angel

Who knew my e-reader was a portal to another galaxy? Now I'm stuck with a fierce alien commander who wants to claim me as his own.

Contemporary Romance

Royal Bad Boy

I'm not falling in love with my arrogant, annoying, sex god boss. Nope. No way.

Royally Fake Fiancé

The Duke of New Arcadia has an image problem only a fiancé can fix. And I'm the lucky lady he's chosen to play Cinderella.

Beauty & The Lumberjacks

After this logging season, I'm giving up sex. For...reasons.

Her Marine Daddy

My hot Marine hero wants me to call him daddy...

Her Dueling Daddies

Two daddies are better than one.

Innocence: dark mafia romance with Stasia Black

I'm the king of the criminal underworld. I always get what I want. And she is my obsession.

Beauty's Beast: a dark romance with Stasia Black

Years ago, Daphne's father stole from me. Now it's time for her to pay her family's debt...with her body.

About Renee Rose

USA TODAY BESTSELLING AUTHOR RENEE ROSE loves a dominant, dirty-talking alpha hero! She's sold over two million copies of steamy romance with varying levels of kink. Her books have been featured in USA Today's *Happily Ever After* and *Popsugar*. Named Eroticon USA's Next Top Erotic Author in 2013, she has also won *Spunky and Sassy's* Favorite Sci-Fi and Anthology author, *The Romance Reviews* Best Historical Romance, and has hit the USA Today list fifteen times with her Bad Boy Alphas, Chicago Bratva, and Wolf Ranch series.

Renee loves to connect with readers!
www.reneeroseromance.com
reneeroseauthor@gmail.com

About Lee Savino

Lee Savino is a USA today bestselling author, mom and chocoholic.

Warning: Do not read her Berserker series, or you will be addicted to the huge, dominant warriors who will stop at nothing to claim their mates.

I repeat: Do. Not. Read. The Berserker Saga.

Download a free book from www.leesavino.com (don't read that either. Too much hot, sexy lovin').